MW00578991

LoveQuest

By

Pamela Jean Horter-Moore

Book design by Pamela Jean Horter-Moore
Front Cover Image: © Mike Heywood | Dreamstime.com
Back Cover Image: © Alfonsodetomas | Dreamstime.com
Back Cover Photograph: Christopher Burton Moore

Pamela Jean Horter-Moore
This is a work of fiction. Any resemblance to anyone living or dead is entirely coincidental.

Visit my website at www.PamelaHorter-Moore.com

Printed in the United States of America
First Printing: February 2017
Published by Orchid Star Publishing

ISBN: 978-1-62747-050-6
Ebook ISBN: 978-1-62747-027-8

Dedicated to:

My cousin Patricia Ann Schachern,

who believed in me from the beginning

and

My niece Jean Marie Horter

who was the first to read my story

Chapter One

The Oracle

Many years ago in a distant land, there existed a wise oracle. It took no human form, being the source of a tranquil pool of water that issued from the depths of a chasm. At some time in the distant past, the oracle had been nothing more than a spring, a bubbling oasis often overlooked by weary travelers.

Then one day, the god Apollo wandered by, having secretly taken on mortal guise to view the construction of his temple some miles back along the path. No one who looked at him that day would have thought Apollo was a god. To disguise himself, he had dressed in a cloth tunic and goat-hide britches. He had taken on the aspect of an ordinary old man with a weathered face and wrinkled brow, ensuring that he would receive no notice from passers-by. As he made his way on foot alone over the public pathway, stirring the hot, dry dust with his feet and walking staff, Apollo became very thirsty. He stopped at the public waterhole but discovered to his dismay that it had dried up. He considered abandoning his disguise to call up water with his divine powers when he heard the gurgle of water in the chasm below. He carefully picked his way down through the rocks and discovered a shallow pool seeping from the dark underground. When he bent his head to slake his thirst, he found that the water was cool and refreshing. Rising to his feet, he saluted the spring and said, "Faithful water, a salvation to the fatigued of body and spirit, I grant you the gift of speech and prophecy, and the power of discernment and knowledge in the ways of humankind, that you may shed truth to the deluded, comfort to the traveler, and enlightenment to the seeker." With that, Apollo struck the ground with his staff, and an immortal presence was born in the depth of the water, possessing such wisdom and fair judgment that future travelers were drawn to it. As the oracle shared its gift with all wanderers, its fame spread across the land so that many journeyed to find relief and peace or to seek advice and counsel in its dark water. If they approached the oracle respectfully, they might receive the answers they desired, gain comfort, and return home refreshed.

To make such a journey, pilgrims were willing to accept risks. Scoundrels and highwaymen, as well as the pious, took this route. The road passed through areas that bristled with mystery and magic. Stories of pilgrims who had witnessed giants, unicorns, and harpies at certain points along the way accompanied the drinks in the tavern and the evenings spent around the fireplaces of the travel lodges. These were people who believed in legend, who had faith in things unknown and sublime. In their universe, there was room for angels and demons, spirits and fairies, satyrs and centaurs, and all the creatures of folklore. There was room for an Ultimate Creator, whose plan was so immense that it required only faith or lack of faith. There was room also for heroes and heroines, and for immortal individuals who appeared in human form but possessed far greater powers. Humans in their innocence called them gods, but it was really the Ultimate Creator who had set these immortal beings over humankind to guide the people during their infancy. These gods made their homes far above the villages that people built, on Mount Olympus and other high mountaintops rising closer to heaven than humankind could ever aspire.

During this time of mystery and superstition, this oracle of the immortal Apollo was one of many soothsayers, competing with priests, prophets, wizards, and gypsies who were mostly incompetent, inaccurate, or motivated by a desire for fortune or fame. These humbugs revealed their prophecies in riddles and puzzles, or in oblique messages, but Apollo commissioned the oracle to succinctly carry divine messages and predictions of the future. It supplied answers to all those who were brave enough to make the journey. It made no judgment on the merits of the question; it was way above that triviality. However, it was always most happy to answer questions dealing with love, and, remembering Apollo's great gift of immortality, ever eager to ingratiate itself to the gods when they requested its help.

On this particular day, the wealthy cloth merchant Pericles and his wife Leena were making their way toward the oracle with their three daughters, Medea, Tanna, and Psyche. As was his custom when he journeyed to the oracle, Pericles had hired an elegant coach for his womenfolk and a fine horse for himself. Being a prudent man as well as rich, he had also hired a couple of mercenaries as bodyguards to protect them along the way.

Pericles rode at the head of his party, straddling a beautiful snow-white gelding on a leather saddle trimmed in precious stones. Although he was past his prime as a middle-aged man with graying hair and a pot-belly, he knew he still cut an impressive figure in his feathered cap, scarlet coat trimmed in fur, woolen leggings, and high leather boots shined to a gloss. He had always remembered his mentor's words, often repeated during his apprenticeship in Phoenicia: Clothes make the man, my boy. One has to keep up appearances. One must live up to his station and be the object of admiration for his fine dress and regal deportment. Pericles had been a good apprentice, and had first managed his master's shop in Philandria before buying him out there and establishing outlets in Athens and Sparta. Yes indeed, he had come far in the world and was deserving of the comforts success had given him. Now Pericles sat straight in the saddle, looking ahead with the demeanor that he hoped suggested his extreme piety as well as his high status. There was nothing he liked better than a pilgrimage to the oracle. Although it took him away from his thriving businesses, he enjoyed traveling, making and renewing friendships, and impressing passers-by with his prosperity.

Pericles was a regular visitor, being a religious and insecure man trusting in the oracle's renowned wisdom. However, on this occasion, he was not seeking answers for himself, but for his three daughters, each of whom had passed the first bloom of youth. Living in a time and in a community where women had few options, Pericles expected his daughters to marry. After all, he reasoned, it is traditional that sons and daughters marry. And if the Pericles family was anything, it was traditional.

His wife Leena sat uncomfortably in the front seat of the coach with their youngest daughter Psyche. Although the cushions beneath her were plump and luxurious, Leena couldn't share her husband's ease. She didn't like to travel and would have preferred to stay home, where the surroundings were familiar and the risk of danger minimal.

This coach, made from the finest oak and trimmed in gold, was an extravagance she could have done without. The hiring of that gelding and those mercenaries was a waste of money. Even worse, this unnecessary and expensive display might tempt highwaymen, and those mercenaries really didn't look as though they were tough enough to survive an ambush if it happened along the way. And what was so wrong with their own coach that he had to hire this one? She didn't like it. It attracted too much attention. Why an open coach? She didn't want everyone looking at her and her daughters. She liked her privacy. She had tried to convince Pericles that their own coach was good enough, but he didn't listen. He never listened to her. He said: "Woman, you worry too much. Now you just make an appointment at Penelope's Bath and Spa and have them dress up your hair. I won't have my wife looking like a middle-class frump!" So instead of her salt-and-pepper hair being smoothed into a simple bun, as she preferred to wear it, she had this towering mass secured with hairpins and lacquer. Instead of her simple gown and apron, she wore a brilliant blue gown made out of a material that rustled with every step she took. She was far too old and plump to be wearing something like this. Another one of his ideas! In her mind, Leena brought up a calendar. How many days had they been gone? How many days until they were back home? She was keeping count.

Pericles' and Leena's two other daughters sat in the back seat of the coach. Medea, the elder of the two, was a thin and dark girl whose sharp nose, narrow face, and piercing black eyes gave her the appearance of a bird of prey. Her unadorned straight black hair fell to her shoulders. Her gown was brown and quite simple, but it was made from the finest material her father could buy, and the glittering dangle of medallions, awards and prizes won in mathematics and science competitions hanging around her neck and wrists compensated for the otherwise plainness of her dress. Medea had endured the journey with irony, regarding her father's faith as superstition. She herself was far too educated and logical to believe in gods, oracles, or prophecies. There was little to believe, and those who did were fools. She considered it her lot in life to point out the stupidity she saw all around her, except that she kept silent in regard to her parents. She held both of them in contempt – one for the control that he had over her and the other for her docility, but Pericles gave her a generous allowance and often flattered her by introducing her as his "smart one."

Medea was glad to sit in the back seat of the coach with her sister Tanna, who, though so different from her in every way, possessed the same icy tongue and disdain for humanity. Along the way, they often shared snide comments in muffled voices, snickering to themselves.

Tanna lounged in her seat, pressing her generous flesh into the sumptuous cushions beneath her. Her hair, currently dyed blonde, was dressed much like her mother's, in a towering hive of ringlets and lacquer, but this suited her. Her father didn't have to persuade her to make an appointment at Penelope's Bath and Spa for the entire program – massage, sauna, hair, manicure, and makeup. Even now, days after the treatment, her plump face was still made up like that of a porcelain doll. The rich red material of her gown clung to her as she reclined, following the folds of fat on her belly and thighs. The neckline of her gown plunged to reveal an ample cleavage, which she showed to best advantage, hoping to catch the eyes of some fine young man. She had begun the trip with zest, eager to shop in the towns along the way and enjoy the exuberant atmosphere of the travelers' inns, where she might find a companion to entertain her for an evening. Tanna and her new lover would exchange caresses and promises of more intimate encounters before her father beckoned her to come in for the night. Because she was "the life of the party," always fun-loving, pleasure-seeking, and attracting attention to herself, Pericles smiled and nodded indulgently, saying that she was his "merry one." Now, however, as they approached the purpose of their journey, Tanna was grumpy and restless. These matters of faith were simply too boring!

Sitting in the front seat with her mother and dressed in pink ruffles that made her look much younger than she was, Psyche, the youngest daughter, shared her mother's embarrassment at being in such a prominent position in an open coach. She knew her father had placed her in the front so that he could show her off to all passers-by. She was the beauty of the family, having shining locks of ash-brown hair that flowed to the middle of her back, and doe-like hazel eyes. Her face bore such charm and refinement that she turned heads wherever she went and was the prized guest of honor at every hometown festival and celebration.

Being a celebrity didn't make Psyche happy. Neither the accolades of the people nor the doting attention of her parents meant more to her than her sisters' rejection. They never liked her, and even now Psyche knew she was the object of much of their mirth as they sat behind her in the coach. She could hear them muttering to each other during the journey and was sad to think that she would never share the friendship that Medea and Tanna had with each other. She would always be an outcast, unwanted, and unloved.

However, Psyche was an obedient daughter who derived pleasure in making her parents happy. It was in that spirit that she had made the journey to the oracle. She didn't question her father's faith but neither did she give much credence to it. Her presence before the oracle was a matter of duty to her parents, so she accepted it with joy.

She thought, *I don't know about oracles and prophecies. There are people like my father who accept without doubt the order of the universe as it has been explained to us by our priests and priestesses. I've thought about faith for a long time. I've listened to Medea's views; they are so cold and precise. She even dares to say there is no Ultimate Creator! How can there be no Creator when there is so much beauty in the world? Why, then, is there such a variety in the plant and animal kingdoms? Nothingness could not create these, but an artist could. Sometimes, though, I wonder.*

Psyche stopped her thoughts. As they rode closer to the oracle, the traffic on the highway became heavier. She saw travelers on foot, on horseback, and in coaches much like the one in which they were riding. She was hoping that an entourage of royalty or nobility might pass, as had happened a couple of years before when a prince of Athens rode by with his attendants. She had enjoyed that experience. She had not even minded when the military police stopped all traffic and delayed their travel. She knew that her father had enjoyed the delay as well, even though he pretended to complain about the lost time. How he glowed and stuck out his chest when the prince rode by! Ever since, Psyche had heard him tell his friends over and over, "The prince saluted me as I stood in the crowd on my way to the oracle." Tanna had enjoyed the splendor as much as Psyche, but Leena and Medea had no use for pomp and circumstance. Leena was silently fretting about the delay and Medea was muttering curses at all princes and the forces who supported them.

Once again, Psyche was interrupted as the entrance to the oracle came into view. She silently counted the number of times she had been to the oracle. Five. This was six. With every visit, the entrance to the oracle and the grounds surrounding it seemed to change. She could recall when there was nothing but a little park. At that time, a pilgrim merely tied his horse to a post and approached the oracle on foot without fanfare. Now, however, valets waited for the more prosperous pilgrims at the entrance of the grotto, while attendants assured lesser travelers that their horses and wagons were safe in the lot in front of the entrance. Merchants set up temporary booths to take advantage of the warm season, selling food, drink, and souvenirs. Others had set up concessions with amusements and games of skill and chance. Pony rides were also available for the children. The last time they had come, someone had set up a carriage to ferry visitors to the oracle so as to avoid the walk from the entrance. Psyche knew her father Pericles loved the hustle and bustle of people and commerce.

"Here we are!" he announced, rubbing his hands together gleefully and dismounting his horse. He dismissed the mercenaries and spoke importantly to the valet concerning the disposition of his transportation before helping his wife and daughters from the coach. He and Leena argued about renting a carriage so that she could ride instead of walk down to the oracle; her knee joints were acting up again, but he was set against it. He did not want to deny his family the reverent walk through the park to the grotto.

Once again, Leena gave in, and Psyche suspected that spiritual wellbeing was not Pericles' real reason for turning down a carriage. He loved to strut at the head of the family, looking all about him to make sure they were noticed. He was especially pleased when he came upon someone he knew. Then it would be, "Why hello, Timons, fancy meeting you here! Who is that, your wife? I could have guessed. Didn't you tell me she was the prettiest girl in Attica? Ha, ha! Are the children with you? No? So Sappho is taking up the priesthood and Nestor is at the academy? Who is he studying under?

That fellow? Oh, I hear he's a trouble-maker." And then it would be, "By the way, Timons, I'd like you to meet my own lovely lady. Yes, Leena and I have been married for twenty-five years. This is our eldest, Medea. She'd give that crazy professor a runaround or two, I can tell you that. Here's our middle child, Tanna. She's a lively girl, full of fun. And here is our darling Psyche." Her father's friend would pause over the face of each girl and grow warm at the sight of Psyche. "What a lovely child!"

"Oh yes," Pericles would say. "She's our gem. Our sweet jewel." As the family moved on, Medea and Tanna would let their parents take the lead, pinching and poking Psyche and trying to trip her up. "Oh yes. She's our gem all right!" they would cackle.

This hurt Psyche's feelings. She never asked these people to make a fuss over her. Even now, she could feel the eyes on her and knew she was part of the reason why her father insisted on walking rather than taking the carriage. He loved showing her off. She must smile when she didn't feel like smiling and return compliments graciously. Sometimes she believed her beauty was more of a curse than a blessing. How could she ever be sure if people liked her for her beauty or for herself? Why did she always have to be on display? When she was honored as Queen of the Festival merely by her presence at a farmer's market, she couldn't tell her admirers that she didn't feel good and didn't want to glow and smile. Her sisters were not nearly as lovely as she and they paid her back by being mean to her. They didn't understand the burden it was to be beautiful.

The family had passed the tacky concessions lining the entrance to the park. Now within the gates, they saw picnickers relaxing under the trees and heard the raucous laughter of children and young people at play. Once beyond the picnic area, the following sign greeted the pilgrims:

This is holy ground.
Your devout silence is appreciated.

As the family approached, conversation faded and men slowly plucked hats from their heads. Psyche looked around at the carefully manicured gardens that graced this part of the park. Placards indicated this garden was dedicated to Ares, the god of War, by the widow of General Ajax while that one was dedicated to Athena, the goddess of Wisdom, by the Athens Garden Club. Many other gods and goddesses were named. Of course, at the center of this display was the garden to Apollo, the one who established the oracle here and gave it its power. This was one way in which the people honored the super beings who lived on nearby Mount Olympus and gained their favor. These gods were very powerful but very capricious. It would have been considered presumptuous to try to gain the Ultimate Creator's favor by way of gifts and honors. Besides, the Ultimate Creator couldn't be bribed. At the edge of the gardens, a copse appeared, sheltering the final pathway to the oracle. Pericles and his family were especially silent walking the narrow descent to the bubbling pool below. As they walked, they passed pilgrims on their return journey. Their faces were either lit with joy and peace, or bleak with despair and weeping. How Psyche sympathized with their sorrow! Her mother warned her not to grieve too much for them, or she might curse her own destiny.

Now Psyche could see the oracle. Her father's step quickened. He ran as if he were meeting an old friend. The oracle appeared simply as a pool of water springing up from the depths of the earth. Although the pool was sheltered by a rim of rock on all sides, beds of ferns, arrowheads, mallows, bedstraws, and lilies grew abundantly around its edge. When Psyche had been much younger, one approached the oracle on the knees. Now, however, someone had placed benches near the pool, aiding the elderly and infirm. The oracle didn't seem to mind. It was really a very pretty place. Contemplation, however, was out of the question, since the oracle was always busy listening to supplicants and then moving them on.

The last pilgrim had just risen from her knees. She was a middle-aged woman who seemed to grow older as she considered the words of the oracle. She pulled her shawl more closely around her, straightened herself and left, her eyes cast down and averted. Pericles strode up confidently to take her place.

"Pericles and family, come forward," commanded a deep voice. The voice always startled Psyche, echoing as it did around the rim of rocks. An eerie light appeared at the bottom of the pool and flickered across the walls of the cavern. This could be a terrible experience for the timid. Even the bold could not help but be impressed.

Pericles groveled at the brink of the pool. "Oh great oracle, seer of the future and past. It has been two years since my last visit," he said.

"Don't you think I know that?" the oracle replied impatiently. The oracle had always found Pericles' self-importance and love of drama annoying, but it was so moved by his childlike faith that it treated him like a stern father treats his dull schoolboy. "Pericles," the oracle said in a kinder tone, "why have you come to visit me now?"

"I seek nothing for myself, oh wise one," Pericles responded. "As you prophesized, I have prospered in the garment trade. I now own one of the largest shops in Philandria, with outlets in Athens and Sparta. Let me thank you once again, oh wise one, for persuading me from joining the priesthood so many years ago. Nor do I seek anything for my wife here who has been richly endowed by my successes.

No, I come to you for my children, my three daughters. They are becoming of an age when decisions must be made."

Pericles' voice echoed away on a supplicating note. The oracle was silent. The eerie light flickered more quickly. It seemed a very long time before the oracle spoke, and when it did, everyone's heart was racing.

"Let me assure you that your daughters will get what they deserve," replied the voice. "I've had ample opportunity from past visits to gauge what manner of women they are. Your eldest sneers at this. She likens me to a magician and you to a buffoon. Let knowledge, science, and cynicism be her lifelong companions; she'll find them cold comfort! Your middle child is the exact opposite, but her passions are coarse and vulgar. She is a creature of shallow interests. She has sought after pleasure and ease, and she shall find them. However, hers is a thirst that is never quenched, even in the lap of plenty. These daughters shall marry compatible men. I see good fortune for them. Fortune as the world defines it, I mean."

The oracle went silent as if it had forgotten Psyche, but it was instead gauging her melancholy, self-doubt and self-loathing, marveling at her disdain for the gifts she had been given. The long stretch of silence troubled Psyche and her parents.

"The youngest daughter is a very special woman," said the oracle. "There must be a great destiny for her, because I see less clearly. She has great beauty, but she is less beautiful than she might be because she takes all her blessings for granted. What I see for her future is very erratic and confusing – rather like the feelings and emotions I read from her now. Here is your deep one, Pericles! She has indeed been marked for destiny. She will make a marvelous marriage to....now this is terribly unclear. It looks as if the husband will not be human. Some fantastic creature, surely, but not human. Never mind. It's to be a great marriage!"

The oracle paused. The family of Pericles hesitated, waiting for more. "Well?" prompted the oracle. "What else can I do for you today?"

"Not human!" squeaked Leena, the hair rising on her head.

"Oh cheer up, woman!" rebuked the oracle crossly. "I said it was going to be a marvelous marriage, didn't I?" The oracle was familiar with people like Leena. People who would go hungry at a banquet for fear the food was tainted. People whose worry stopped them from taking the great risks in life that are necessary for growth and progress. Behind the Pericles family, the oracle could see other pilgrims were waiting. It was time to move on. "That's all I see for your children today," declared the oracle. "You're a lovely family, and I'm sorry, but I have no more insights. Goodbye for now. Goodbye. Come back in a year or two and try me again."

The oracle fell silent. The interview was over. Quaking, the Pericles family turned to go. "Not human!" Leena muttered in dismay. Medea and Tanna exchanged smirks. Psyche felt dizzy and bewildered. The oracle's words had shaken her. Her father braced her with his arm. "Come, my pet," he said. "You will make a marvelous, marvelous marriage!"

"Oh, this is all too dear!" exclaimed Medea in disgust. She turned her back to her father and youngest sister and stepped ahead of the others. Tanna caught up with her, boiling with rage and envy.

"That charlatan! That fraud!" she hissed. "Shallow, coarse and vulgar, am I?'

"Hold off your anger until we can talk privately," Medea whispered.

14

Seeing that Psyche was steady, Pericles once again strode to the head of the party. As he walked past, Medea wondered whether he would ask her to explain the oracle's comment about her considering him a buffoon, but he had already forgotten. He was too busy thinking about how he must look to the strangers around him: quite handsome and fit for a man in his senior years, dressed in a fashionable and expensive outfit and leading a procession of women dressed equally well. He saw himself as a devout pilgrim, reverently leading his family on a tour of the gardens.

Leena scurried to catch up with him, while Medea and Tanna fell behind their parents. They made it clear they didn't want Psyche's company. They wouldn't let her come abreast of them. The family was still in a restricted area and talk was forbidden, but now that Pericles had moved ahead, Medea and Tanna felt free to whisper. It didn't matter if Psyche overheard.

"Why do we have to spend every vacation here?" whined Tanna. "That oracle never has anything interesting to say. And who can believe what it says anyway? If it were truthful, it would see my attributes." She considered the words of the oracle once more and mellowed. "I'm sure, though, that the oracle is perfectly correct in saying I shall find pleasure and ease, and that I shall lie in the lap of plenty. And I'm sure it's equally true that I (and you too, of course, Medea) shall marry compatibly and have good fortune. So I guess that this visit wasn't totally wasted."

"Yes, the oracle said all those things," Medea replied, "but don't fool yourself as Father does. This oracle is a delusion. I can't figure out how it's being operated, but I know I could find out if I considered it the least bit interesting. This is a sideshow attraction, nothing more. The people who operate the oracle are very unimaginative and mediocre. They tell people exactly what they expect to hear.

15

They have to give them a little good news and a little bad news to keep it believable and have them coming back. There are people like me and you who know better, but come anyway. And then there are people like our father. Just watch him throw his money into the donation box at the end of the walk! These are the fools who make the people who own the oracle very rich. I wonder how much those merchants have to pay to operate the concessions. I wonder whether they're made to give a percentage of what they earn to the corporation operating in the interests of those who own the oracle. I wonder how much money they make in a season."

These questions had no interest for Tanna, but she agreed just the same. "How right you are, sister. The people who operate the oracle accused me of being coarse and vulgar, but it is they who display their common taste. Like the yahoos and morons from our village, they pick up on the very average looks of our sister and mark her out as something special."

"Right! And remember how the oracle hesitated? All for effect. I'll say one thing for the person who speaks for the oracle – he's a great actor."

"When you come right down to it, what did the oracle really say about Psyche?"

"That she's beautiful and deep. Hah! That she will make a marvelous marriage to something that is not human." Medea complained, "Psyche deep? That's a good one! She can hardly say two words for herself. It's the same with all these pretty girls. If I gave her a penny for her thoughts, I'd expect some change back," she snickered.

"I like the part about her marriage," said Tanna. "It becomes not a matter of whom she marries but what she marries. What do you think it will be, sister? Animal, vegetable, or mineral?"

16

Psyche wanted to cry. It wasn't the words that hurt. It was the venomous way in which her sisters spoke them. They didn't love her. She sometimes thought they hated her. She wanted very much for them to accept her. She tried to master her hurt. She was used to them being mean to her. It was because she was beautiful that they scorned her. Did they think she chose to be beautiful? Did they think she really liked being displayed by their father? Did they think she enjoyed the attention of the villagers?

How her sisters relished the oracle's prophecy regarding her marriage! Strangely, having recovered from her initial reaction, Psyche felt nothing at all. Although she was not as cynical and incredulous as Medea, she likewise put little faith upon the oracle. Yes, it was true that its advice often seemed correct, but encouraging her father to pursue the merchant's trade rather than go into the priesthood didn't take divine revelation. Was it necessarily divine assistance that led to her father's success as a businessman? And what about the dramatic quality of the oracle's message, which raised more questions than it answered? What was "not human?" That could mean something or nothing at all.

To try to forget about the oracle and her sisters, Psyche focused her attention upon the gardens. Each was prepared with love and devotion, but toward what? The first was to Ares the god of War, as dedicated by General Ajax's widow. What gratitude had she toward the god of War? Certainly, it had made a good career for her husband and she had prospered by it, but it was war that had widowed her. And not just once. She was doomed to widowhood when she married. Not by death, but by one campaign after another, which took her husband out of the house and far from her. Before the statue of the warrior god stood two lines of red and white rose bushes, facing off like soldiers before a battle.

A semi-circle of palm trees surrounded the statue like a group of adoring worshippers. Psyche had no affection for the god of War. No other god demanded such bloody sacrifice. Of all the super beings on Mount Olympus, he was the most cruel, and yet he existed only because of his place in the human breast. The two-year old boy, clutching a dolly in one hand, picks up a stick with the other. Soon the dolly is abandoned for more sticks, and stones, knives, spears, swords, bows and arrows. This is the quest for manhood that grieves all mothers. The waste of life and energy could not be reconciled with monuments and medals, by parades and by words of nationalism and honor. In relief, Psyche moved on to catch up with her family.

The second garden was dedicated to Demeter, the goddess of the Harvest. Here fruits, vegetables, and grains of all kinds had been planted. The garden had prospered; every plant appeared to be exactly at the point at which it should be for the season. As practical and nourishing as this garden was, its beauty was most becoming. Plump fruits and vegetables hanging from trees, vines, and stocks were rich in colors of green, red, gold and purple. The grains rippled and swayed gracefully with each breeze. At the center of the garden, the statue of Demeter balanced a basket of fruit on her shoulder and another of grain at her hip. Despite her lack of faith, Psyche couldn't restrain a thrill of adoration toward the mother of plenty who labored to preserve the work of the Ultimate Creator.

Next was the garden dedicated to Athena, the goddess of Wisdom. It was well-ordered, with sculptured flower beds leading to a statue of the goddess, crooking a book in her arms, an owl perched on her right shoulder. Although the garden bore the distinctive mark of discipline, the flowers were chosen for their bright and joyful colors. Psyche revered the goddess of Wisdom and would have expected a similar respect from Medea, whose love of learning was widely acknowledged at the academy. Medea, however, considered herself beyond the favor of Athena. Under her critical and analytical eyes, the super beings at Mount Olympus shrank to microscopic proportions. Even the Ultimate Creator was subject to her scrutiny. Was Medea wise to dismiss wonder and inspiration from her studies, or did wisdom require much more than knowledge?

Because he was thought to be the lord of the oracle, Apollo's garden was the centerpiece of the park. His gold-plated statue was rubbed to a shine. It depicted him as a man in his prime years, with a composed brow and a body still hard and lean. Here was the god to whom were attributed the finer instincts of humankind. The garden was well-ordered, but suggested a passion borne of inspiration. The walls at one end of the garden stood clean, straight, and spartan above a fragrant mass of hyacinths. At the other end of the garden, the walls were ornate with friezes celebrating the god's history, and a clutch of reeds surrounded a curved and shallow pool. The landscapers here hadn't wished to let the intent of their work be missed: A large stone scroll at the exit of the garden exhorted the pilgrims to wisely use their gifts and thereby seek perfection.

The garden dedicated to Aphrodite, the goddess of Beauty, was landscaped and gracefully designed. Whereas the garden of Athena was simple and orderly, this garden was elegant and sensual. Behind the delicate statue of Aphrodite was a wall fashioned with slender white columns. Before this wall was a pool of goldfish and water lilies. Several birch saplings grew in the remote areas of the garden. At the center sprang a fountain. Here the air was heavy with roses. How spectacular were the colors of the plump blossoms that grew on the bushes surrounding it! Each rose seemed to represent a lovely and sensual woman, dressed in her most dazzling gown, striving to give pleasure to the beholder. Off to the side of the garden were less glorious and simple herbs and plants such as jasmine, honeysuckle, chamomile, lavender, heather and chicory. Psyche broke away from her family and roamed the garden alone, letting its beauty command her senses. She didn't try to examine its meaning and apply its message to her own life. She merely relished this solitary moment and the opportunity to be sheltered and made anonymous by something more lovely than herself.

Her sisters' envious giggles disrupted her reverie. In sudden anger, she looked over her right shoulder and saw them looking at the statue of Aphrodite. She didn't turn her head fast enough to avoid their glances and was dismayed when they began to walk in her direction.

"I thought you might be interested in comparing yourself with the statue of Aphrodite," commented Tanna. "It's a close enough resemblance; it has all your wit and personality."

"All day long it stands and waits for admirers. Admirers come, but they never stay. As time goes by, the wind and weather erode its beauty, but it remains a good target for bird droppings," added Medea.

Psyche turned from them and hid her face in her hands. Tears jumped to her eyes as if a spring had been tapped. She heard Tanna snicker "She's crying," as she began running toward the exit of the garden.

Her sisters did not run after her. They were especially unconcerned because it was obvious that neither parent had witnessed the scene. An excuse could be made for Psyche's disappearance. She wouldn't go far and she didn't dare tell her parents what her sisters had said, for fear of more torment.

Psyche ran out of the garden of Aphrodite and sought refuge in the garden dedicated to Eros, the god of Love. She hid behind the statue at the far end of the garden and tried to compose herself. She cursed the beauty that was a barrier between her and her sisters, and tried to convince herself that Medea was wrong. Seated at the base of the statue, she peered up through her tears at the composed and harmonious features of the youthful god of Love. This was what she sacrificed for beauty. With her beauty came no love, no joy. Just separation from others.

She could see the other members of her family now entering the garden. They stopped to enjoy the sensual colors and textures of the flowers beyond the gate. Here, there was a sense of wonderful disorder, of delight and passion. The smell of honeysuckle was heavy in the air. Irises grew in thick spikes and the fruit was growing heavy on the trees in the small orchard at the corner of the garden. Around the statue grew clumps of violets and buttercups. Psyche had wiped her tears away by the time her family approached. Neither she nor her sisters would look at each other, and the parents didn't ask for an explanation. It was time to go. Quickly, Psyche made a supplication to the statue: Prove them wrong, she silently implored. It was not a prayer, but a cry for mercy.

Chapter Two

The Wrath of Aphrodite

On Mount Olympus, Aphrodite, the goddess of Beauty, had been spending an agreeable morning viewing her mortal protégées through her crystal looking glass as she lounged in her villa. Like her fellow occupants of the holy mountain, she took intense interest in the activities of the human world and enjoyed its admiration and attention. She had made it a practice to visit the birthplace of each child under the gods' dominion to bless it with joy and beauty. Some children she blessed more generously than others, and they were the ones she was looking at now, ready to bless them with more gifts if they were deserving or punish them for their offenses if they were not.

This was what she had been born for. Her mother had birthed her in a bed of coral, and her father Zeus had plucked her from the sea to live with him high above the deep. Dropped from his arms on top of Mount Olympus, a new immortal life already in the bloom of womanhood, she had walked naked into her father's palace before the eyes of all the gods, dripping sea water and seaweed, translucent abalone shells glittering in her long black hair as she approached her father's throne. Every gaze was transfixed upon her. Every god wanted her. She did not like to be taken for granted.

So when it was Psyche's turn to be scrutinized by Aphrodite that morning, what the goddess saw in her looking glass made her furious. The conduct of the daughters of Pericles in the garden of the oracle deeply offended her. Although she fumed over Medea's and Tanna's insulting comments about her statue, she was most annoyed by the conduct of Psyche. After all, it was Psyche and not Medea or Tanna whom she had marked for special blessings at birth. Aphrodite was not interested in Medea and Tanna and had resolved many times to spare them her generosity. But ingratitude on the part of a protégée could not be endured. Her rage had been building for some time. Psyche's thoughts and actions today had been the last straw.

She called to her son, Eros. The god of Love was there in an instant because he was a dutiful boy who loved his mother above all creatures. Aphrodite likewise loved him with all the passion a mother could have for an only child.

Before Eros, Aphrodite had felt incomplete, desired by many but caring for no one. Although each of the gods had longed to make her his wife, her father Zeus had married her to Hephaestus, Blacksmith to the gods, in repayment for his good service. Hephaestus was the ugliest of the gods, a twisted, lame creature who was more comfortable with his molten metal and bellows than with the loveliest of all goddesses. In retaliation for the mismatch, Aphrodite sought lovers among the gods and mortals, easily bored and constantly moving on to the next conquest. Then one night in a dream, she was visited by a magnificent creature who was not quite a bird and yet not quite a man, with a soft feathered breast and large and glorious wings as white and as light as snow. All night long in her dream state, he came to her again and again, insatiable in his passion, his wings beating over her and caressing her body. He was her Dream Lover. But when the dawn came, he was gone. Never to return. A mystical being born on that night and dying with the light, he existed only for the hours of lovemaking he had enjoyed in her arms.

Aphrodite had been ready to give in to her grief for his departure when she noticed a large alabaster egg in the place where her lover had lain. As she admired the egg's beauty and the perfection of its smooth surface and symmetry, there was a great hatching sound, and a lovely male child with delicate white wings emerged from its shell. His curly black hair framed an exquisite face that left no doubt who his mother was, and his melting brown eyes were fringed by long curling dark lashes.

Aphrodite knew that the child Eros was a consolation gift from her mysterious lover, a reminder of their brief encounter. Therefore, she treasured him and raised him jealously, rarely letting him out of her sight for too long. She could deny Eros nothing and gladly spent one night with her forsaken husband Hephaestus in return for his forging a bow and quiver of arrows that was Eros' heart's desire.

Upon grasping the bow and placing the quiver of arrows on his shoulder, Eros transformed the tools into instruments of his power – not made of metal, but made of something that could be just as fatal: Forevermore, the god of Love would be associated with the bow and arrow. He had found a way to wound his prey. He could now take his place among the gods and goddesses of Mount Olympus.

And so now, Eros stopped what he was doing to answer his mother's summons. He was just in the first bloom of youth, beardless, with downy hair just beginning to sprout on his chest and upper lip. He was joyful and lively as all young people should be, using his graceful and splendid wings to fly here and there, sometimes full of mischief and sometimes full of good will and affection. His beloved bow and quiver were always on hand, and at his waist were two flasks of water. One flask held sweet water, while the other flask held bitter. By using these waters, he could determine the effect of the arrows on his target.

He was interrupting a very eventful morning to attend his mother's summons. He had been busy spreading love all over the earth and sky. He placed it in a rose by the wayside, a comfort to the traveler. He placed it in a warm loaf of bread, fresh from the oven of a mother's kitchen. He placed it in the hearts of an elderly couple who had no one but each other. He placed it in a mother nursing her newborn child. He placed it in the very first kiss that young boys and girls share when they discover each other. Since his specialty was erotic love, his favorite exploit this morning had been the liaison between a herder and a milkmaid. Neither would get much work done that day. Fortunately, Eros knew that their employer was an affable man who could forgive love's indiscretion. Not all of his exploits had such happy endings.

Aphrodite drew him near and beckoned him to peer into her looking glass. "Take a look at the girl in pink," she directed.

In the mirror, the family of Pericles appeared, journeying from their trip to the oracle. Eros easily picked out Psyche. "Very pretty, Mother," he commented.

"Yes, I have given her many gifts," Aphrodite replied. "But she has received them insultingly. I've put up with her offenses long enough. Tonight I will have my vengeance. I won't take one gift away from her. Instead, I want you to discipline the ingrate. That's why I've asked you to come to me now while her sins are still fresh in my mind."

Eros was puzzled. "What has she done, Mother?" he asked.

"I have always had too tender a heart for these mortals," Aphrodite complained. "Day after day, I'm breaking off from my own business to attend to some matter in the villages below. I go out of my way to bless some of these mortals and receive only their scorn as a reward. Take this mortal Psyche here. I intended her to serve as one of my protégées; I gave her every chance and every opportunity to do me honor.

"Instead, she has shown me offense by disparaging the gifts I have given her. I've been disappointed with her for a long time. Now the very sight of her disgusts me. Do you see those young women who walk in front of her? They are her sisters, and their approval means more to her than all her blessings. The eldest holds me in contempt, but I don't care. She thinks she will look wise if she looks ugly. She'll be a bitter crone before middle age is over. I don't have to put a curse on her to know that. The other girl smears her looks with self-indulgence, and thus devalues herself. There is hope for her if she repents, but that is unlikely. Her mean-spiritedness and shallowness will prevent her redemption. These two are Psyche's mirrors. She has let them define what she is."

Eros remained puzzled. He had seen his mother angry before, but still couldn't grasp the intensity of her outrage. What had this Psyche done to arouse such anger?

"Review my case against the girl!" Aphrodite exclaimed impatiently, sensing his confusion. The images in the mirror shifted to earlier scenes. There was Psyche, wreathed as Queen of the Harvest a year before. She was smiling and surrounded by happy and prosperous people.

"She smiles," said Aphrodite, "but there is no grace or love in that gesture. I know because I read her heart and listened to her conversations with her foolish but faithful father. When he told her to smile for the people, she would ask why. It was too burdensome to be beautiful and accept the joy and pleasure of the villagers. Yet, she smiled because she wanted to please her father, and I can't fault her for that, only for the effort she made to do it. People pay tribute to her beauty all the time. The smiling youths who wish the courage to court her, the women and girls who have extended her their friendship – all have honored me by favoring her. She hates the attention, cannot respond to it with a heartfelt smile, cannot extend the hand in affection, cannot share herself just as that statue in the garden cannot!" Aphrodite stopped, biting back a tirade. But she wasn't finished with her denunciation.

"Psyche was crying in the garden because there was a lot of truth in what her sisters said. As a favored one of mine, however, she should have known in her heart the basis of her sisters' envy and should have understood the nature of their insult to both her and me. I have neither curses nor gifts for them. But she, on the other hand, deserves a fitting punishment. If I disinherited her and made her a hag, she'd be satisfied. So instead I will let her sisters' words be her prophecy. No one but her parents shall love Psyche ever again. She shall continue to have the admiration she finds so oppressive, but no passion shall grow from it. She shall have the beauty of the statue and all of its coldness."

With this, Aphrodite was finished. Eros knew what she was asking him to do. He was always very anxious to do his mother's bidding and he would never think of disobeying her, but these assignments filled him with regret. He found no pleasure in dooming a young woman to loneliness. Nevertheless, he said, "Yes, Mother."

"Tonight," she told him.

"It shall be as you say," said Eros.

He went to the fountains in his mother's garden to refill his flasks of sweet and bitter waters. He made ready his quiver and arrows. Then he waited until nightfall.

Pericles and his family had rented rooms for the night. Being both prosperous and pompous, he had insisted that the innkeeper give him the best available lodgings on the upper floors. He and his wife settled early to bed while his daughters in the other room prepared to do the same. The girls were quiet as they brushed their hair, changed into their bedclothes, and washed away the dirt from the journey. Tanna was still fuming over the visit to the oracle; she and Medea continued to exchange brief comments about it. They said nothing to Psyche, snubbing her for the attention the oracle had paid her. Upon entering the room at the inn, they had both claimed beds and night tables together and forced Psyche to take the bed and night table by the window, which they insisted upon opening to let in the fresh night air. Psyche was pensive, aware of their disfavor and confused over the events of the day.

Eros reverted to invisibility as he flew from Mount Olympus. He quickly found the lodge in which the family was staying and hovered over it. Most of the time, he could shoot his target from a great distance and feel fairly confident about not missing (very strange things could happen if he missed). His intention was to propel an arrow deep into the heart of his victim, causing either passionate love or hatred and loathing depending upon whether the sweet or bitter water had been splashed on his prey or applied to the tip of his arrow. His mother's instructions, however, required a different approach that was less fun and appealing: To deny his victim the passion of his arrows, he must come close to his sleeping prey and place his arrows parallel to her reposing body. An arrow placed parallel to the victim's body could never pierce the heart at all. Then he must sprinkle her with water from the appropriate flask at his waist, and say the words "Let it be so." The sweet water applied with the parallel arrow brought a chaste love which was spent in service to others; the bitter water, however, repelled love and denied service, leaving only destitution and regret. Eros hated this ritual, which doomed his prey to a passionless existence. The fact that the prey was a young and lovely woman didn't make it any easier.

He flew down to the window ledge outside the girls' room and peered inside. They were still awake. He could see Medea already propped up in bed reading, her hair severely drawn away from her face and twisted at the back of her head. Tanna's ample profile was projected on the wall as she rubbed creams and lotions into her skin, watching her reflection in the mirror brightly lit by the candles she had placed on her dressing table. Psyche was staring out the window as she brushed her hair. She was not looking in his direction. Although he was invisible, Eros felt even more uncomfortable. She was very close to him, though unconscious of him. He could have touched her. He saw that she was not only more beautiful than he had first seen, but also more sorrowful. He was suddenly filled with pity. He tried to shake the feeling off, backing away from her.

There was a rustling. Psyche gasped, pulled back from the window and exclaimed to her sisters. "Listen! I hear a noise outside!"

Her voice a mixture of boredom and contempt, Medea broke away from her book to reply, "Of course you do, you fool. This inn is located off a main road. There will be travelers coming and going throughout the night."

"No, I mean up here," Psyche clarified. "Just outside the window."

With a smirk of condescension and amusement, Medea goaded her. "You heard a noise outside a fourth-story window. Now what do you think it could be?"

Psyche considered. "It could be a bird or an insect," she replied. "Or a bat."

"Would you be afraid if it were?"

"I suppose not," Psyche said, becoming defensive. "But that wasn't what I heard. It was more like the sound of someone moving."

"And you find that frightening?"

"Why, yes. It could be a burglar."

"A burglar. And how would a burglar get outside a fourth-story window? With a ladder, a rope or a trellis. Do you see a ladder, a rope or a trellis outside?"

Although she knew she was just feeding her sister's scorn, Psyche leaned out the window and studied the area with care. She really was certain she had heard someone. "No," she answered, ducking back inside.

"Then chances are pretty good that you didn't hear anyone outside," Medea said, adding impatiently, "Really, Psyche. I never did think much of your intelligence, but I didn't think you were that stupid. The visit to the oracle must have rattled what little you have for a brain."

Tanna, tying up her mass of bleached-blonde curls, snorted contemptuously. "You've put your finger right on it, sister. But I'm not sure you've been totally fair to Psyche. A mere human burglar may need ladders and trellises, but you forget that Psyche mixes with more exulted company than we mere mortals. Perhaps it's her future husband paying a call. A fourth-story window would be no problem for a giant or flying dragon."

"Oh yes, I had forgotten Psyche's non-human husband," Medea chortled. "I was just too busy thinking about all the times I've been impressed by her depth. Isn't that what the oracle also said about her? Her comments about fearing a burglar, for instance. They surely make me consider the importance of a good hotel security system."

Rebuffed, Psyche jumped into bed, turned her back to her sisters and pulled the covers over her head. She heard their cruel laughter.

Discovered, Eros was careful to be more quiet. When Psyche had leaned out the window, he sat perfectly still on the ledge, although her face had come so close to his that he could smell her fragrance and feel her warmth. The taunting words of her sisters increased his pity, but he was beginning to understand the nature of Psyche's sin: she let them drag her down and belittle her. She devalued the gifts she was given.

Was that entirely her fault? Eros was developing feelings of antipathy toward her sisters. *I can't do that,* he thought, stopping himself. *I must remain objective. I mustn't care. Why don't they go to sleep so I can finish this?*

He didn't have long to wait. Medea and Tanna went to bed soon after and, tired from the journey, quickly fell asleep. In that instant, Eros was inside the room. He went to Psyche's bedside and gently pulled down the covers to expose her sleeping in her light cotton nightgown. From the top of her head to her toes, she was flawless. He felt such empathy for her that it seemed his heart would burst from pity. It was a shame to deny someone so beautiful, so made for love, its pleasure.

He was, however, obliged to do his mother's will. Psyche's sleep was light and restless, so he thought he should do it quickly. Quietly he took the flask of bitter water from his belt and opened it. Then he took an arrow from his quiver and touched the tip to the bitter water. He laid the arrow alongside Psyche's body. He took another arrow to continue the ritual, splashing drops of bitter water on her head and breasts. Suddenly, the sleeping girl gave a small cry, jerked awake and sat up in bed, looking unconsciously into the face of the unseen youth. Eros was so startled that he pulled back, wounding himself with the arrow he was preparing. Stricken, he was overcome with remorse and had no thought for himself. Instead, he opened the flask of sweet water and spilled it all over Psyche, hoping to diminish the power of the bitter water. With the last drop, he gave Psyche a long look, knowing that something must happen now, something bitter and something sweet. He knew that it would affect him and deal with him as he had dealt with others. Quickly he fled into the night, the blood of the immortals freely flowing from his wound.

Psyche's outcry wakened her sisters. They were surprised to find her drenched with water.

"What happened to you?" inquired Tanna in amazement.

Psyche shook her head in bewilderment. "I don't know. I had a very strange dream. Someone came in through the window and splashed water on me."

Both sisters burst into laughter. When they regained their composure, Medea shook her head. "Tell Father to get the doctor, sister. The trip to the oracle has indeed rattled our sister's brain." She saw Psyche open her mouth to speak and cut her short. "No more. I'm not going to ask any more questions. I don't want to get involved in *that* conversation again!"

"Please no!" groaned Tanna. "Shut up and go to sleep, Psyche!" she growled, burying her head again in her pillow.

Psyche got out of bed and walked to the window. She was beginning to worry. The strangest things seemed to be happening. She wondered if she were going mad. The sounds and the visitation this evening had seemed very real. And yet, they couldn't be. Unless, of course, the oracle's prophecy was beginning to unfold. No human can enter a fourth-story window without tools, a foothold, or assistance. But that was too preposterous. Non-humans and humans didn't marry. Well, not often anyway. For the most part, they avoided each other. Psyche had never even seen one of these extraordinary beings. She wasn't even sure they existed. Medea must be right; she must be suffering delusions. Maybe she would feel more comfortable if she confronted the source of the problem. "May I close the window?" she asked her sisters.

"No!" her sisters chorused. Dejected, Psyche slumped back into bed. The peculiar events of the evening were not repeated.

Eros was weak and nearly fainting when he arrived back on Mount Olympus. His mother's distressed maidservants were the first to see him as he staggered into his mother's garden. With cries of surprise and dismay, they ran to him and surrounded him. He waved them away and they stepped back, staring at him in alarm and amazement. Although he tried to protest, a couple of them turned to get his mother. Throughout the house of Aphrodite the message was passed: the god of Love has been wounded.

Of course the servants were astonished. His kind were believed to be invincible, immortal. But now this. How could it be?

Distraught, Aphrodite came rushing to his side. When she saw Eros, pale, limp and bleeding, hardly able to stand, she gave a great cry and took him in her arms. "My child! My child!" she cried. "How has this happened to you?" She called for her most trusted manservant and directed him to carry her son to bed. She led the way, not wanting Eros to be away from her for an instant.

Once in bed, Eros felt a little stronger. He really didn't think all these ministrations were necessary, but there was no arguing with his mother. She pulled a chair to his bedside and she herself cleaned and dressed his wound.

Eros watched her lovely face as she worked, feeling remorseful when he saw tears cascading down her cheeks. "It's all right, Mother," he said reassuringly. "I'm fine."

"How did this happen?" Aphrodite asked.

"Oh, it was just an accident," replied Eros, trying to dismiss it.

"Accidents like this don't happen to us," said Aphrodite. "Unless they are inflicted by one of our own kind."

"Or by ourselves," added Eros.

Aphrodite was quick to catch his meaning. "You've wounded yourself with one of your arrows, haven't you?" she asked.

Abashed, Eros nodded.

"How did it happen?" she repeated more insistently.

"Do you remember asking me to punish a girl named Psyche?"

In the distress of the moment, Aphrodite had put the matter far back in her mind. She then recalled her earlier conversation with Eros and nodded, beginning to feel even more uneasy.

"She was asleep as I was tending to it. She suddenly woke up and startled me. I drew back and that's when it happened. I pierced myself with one of the arrows I was preparing for her."

In dread, Aphrodite inquired, "Was that all that happened, my child?"

"No," Eros put his hand to his face and averted his eyes. "I've become a victim of my own power."

Aphrodite's eyes were wide with horror. "You've fallen in love with that girl!"

Abashed, he replied, "I'm afraid so."

Aphrodite sprang from the chair and paced back and forth before Eros' bed, wringing her hands. "It's impossible! I won't have it! Bad enough to be human, but to be her! That whining, sniveling little ingrate!"

"Mother, please!" Eros implored. "I can deal with it."

"And just what do you think you're going to do about it?" Aphrodite asked.

Eros shrugged. "Let it run its course, I suppose."

She turned to him. "Oh no you won't! You'll fight this, do you hear me? I'll not give my boy to one who has offended me."

Shrugging his shoulders again, Eros replied, "How can it be helped? I can't reverse my powers, Mother."

"Then I'll find someone who can."

Eros was, of course, well aware of the behavior of those who fell in love. It had been a source of joy and amusement to see how his prey reacted after being struck by one of his swift arrows. Sometimes, however, he saw his victims resist the power of love. How they suffered! He had always been impatient with them. *Give in to it, you fool!* he would think. Now his mother was asking him to resist. He didn't want to.

"I'll take the matter up with my father Zeus immediately," Aphrodite said.

"Please, Mother. Let this run its course," Eros pleaded.

"Absolutely not!" Aphrodite replied firmly. "Honestly, darling. You act almost as if you want to be in love with this hideous girl. I plan to go to my father the moment I leave this room. He'll know what to do." Going to his bedside, she leaned over to pat his hand and kiss his forehead. "You just rest, dear. My servants will be around to make sure that you don't leave your bed."

Eros watched her go, and then glimpsed her attendants who remained in the room. He plainly knew his mother's meaning. Now he was captive in his own bedroom, subject to the fussing of his mother and her over-solicitous followers.

I'm being disciplined as well as nursed, he thought in dismay. He felt somewhat better now, although he was still weak. Eros considered his own feelings and what his mother was asking him to do. He understood the power of his arrows well enough to know that letting love run its course was the quickest way to heal his wound. He also knew that resisting love made the wound much worse. His mother preferred that he resist his love, suffer from his wound, and endure her nursing until he reached the point of objectivity that she expected of him. That required far more self-discipline than he was willing to give. His mother had not been with him when he had visited Psyche at the inn and had experienced her beauty and the warmth and fragrance of her skin. She had not been there when he had heard the taunts of Psyche's sisters and had felt pity for her melancholy. She didn't see her sleeping in bed, her nightgown revealing the tantalizing curves that made his senses swim now. He wanted Psyche and he didn't want to suffer without her. There was no way around it: if he wouldn't resist Psyche, he must resist his mother. Eros was saddened to come to this conclusion. He had always been a most obedient and loyal son. He wouldn't openly resist, for he loved and feared his mother too much to risk a confrontation. Instead, he would resist in subtle and covert ways, using his powers in a fashion even he himself had never tried before.

Zeus had already heard of his grandson's misfortune with the mortal Psyche. There was nothing known by anyone on Mount Olympus that wasn't already known by him. The oldest of all the gods, Zeus was the wisest by reason of his experience and power. He was a tall and mighty old man with white hair that flowed to his shoulders and a lush white beard. His plain white robe hung from one shoulder and reached to his knees. He had no other adornment whatsoever. He needed none. His presence alone was all he needed to command attention. Zeus' blue eyes could glow like steel when he was angry, or dance with mischief when he was joyful. His face usually bore a pleasant expression. He was jovial and good-humored, always ready to laugh. He was capable of sudden anger, but then always ready to forgive a truly contrite offender. He had one big weakness: he was a notorious philanderer, although he was always vowing to reform to please his jealous wife Hera. Zeus did not care for conflict in his own house. Now seated casually on his throne in his private chamber, he listened as his daughter Aphrodite pleaded for a remedy for Eros' wound. Zeus had never seen her so worked up. She was angrier than she had been when he had announced her engagement to Hephaestus before all the gods on Mount Olympus without first consulting her. Zeus knew that a mother will become a tiger when her child is threatened. He also knew that Eros meant everything to his mother. Zeus regretted what he would have to say in reply to her tirade and waited until it was completely over before he made his answer.

"Well, daughter. Let me understand you. Are you asking me to revoke your son's powers?" Zeus asked, staring at her quizzically.

Taken aback, Aphrodite shook her head, surprised he would even suggest such a thing. "No. Of course not. I'm asking a favor just in this one particular instance."

An indulgent father preparing to disappoint a beloved child, Zeus replied, "I understand exactly what you're asking. You're asking me to blot out this occurrence, change Fate and rearrange things to meet your liking," he replied.

Aphrodite exploded. "No, Father, I am asking for nothing of the kind!" Her father's unreasonableness and obtuseness made her bristle. "I'm just asking that you remedy this one single love-spell."

Zeus shook his head. "No dear. I won't do it. This circumstance just doesn't justify it." He changed his tone. "By Mount Olympus, Aphrodite, let the boy experience the consequences of his carelessness! I can't count the times I've had someone of our kind coming to me complaining about that boy. There isn't one god whom he hasn't annoyed with his childish pranks. I've tried to take it all in stride. After all, boys will be boys, and I expect that he's lonely and needing a companion to keep him occupied. But it's about time he grew up a bit and started taking some responsibility for his actions. Well, I can think of nothing better to sober a young man up than a first love affair."

Fuming, Aphrodite said, "My son with that mortal?"

Zeus was unaffected. "Oh come on, now. The girl's not so bad. This accident could benefit her as well. You and I both have loved mortals in our time. Did you see any harm in that?"

Aphrodite was unmoved. She wasn't interested in comparisons with events from her and her father's past. "You know as well as I that there is potential for great harm here."

"There is potential for great harm every time a creature does something extraordinary," Zeus replied. "But I suspect that you are thinking more of yourself than of your son. Now, before you attack me, listen: You are a mother whose only child has been stricken ill, and you are faced with the prospect of sharing your beloved son with another woman. You're not considering my grandson's feelings at all. He's not a small child anymore. He is entitled to that consideration."

"My son is the god of Love!" Aphrodite flung back. "How do you think he feels? Besides, it doesn't matter how he feels about it. He will do as I say. He always has."

Zeus replied, "Is that all that matters? Don't you want him to grow up? We all have free will. We must not obstruct our children from exercising theirs."

Aphrodite rose to her feet, so far out of patience that she forgot Zeus' exulted position. All she understood was that her father was keeping her from having her way. "I didn't come here for a lecture, Father," she said. "If you won't help me, maybe there are others who will!" Without asking his permission to leave, she spun on her heels and stomped out, amazing Zeus with her uncharacteristic behavior.

Aphrodite left Zeus' private chamber in a huff, continuing through her father's palace, hardly noticing the servants who bowed respectfully as she passed. She knew exactly to whom she should speak. If her father wouldn't see reason, her stepmother Hera, the goddess of Marriage and Family, surely would. Aphrodite expected a much more sober assessment of her son's condition from her, counting on Hera's dislike of passionate love outside a chaste and faithful marriage. She found Hera supervising the cleaning in the Great Hall of Zeus' palace. Hera was a great beauty, but always conservative and sensible in her dress. Her brown hair, streaked with silver, was pulled back and hidden under a plain kerchief. Her dove-gray gown of finest linen was covered by a full-length white apron. Under her will, the brooms, dust cloths and mops were flying, doing her bidding as if two dozen servants were moving them. Aphrodite knew that Hera was conscious of her presence, but not ready to acknowledge her, still holding a grudge against her for taking her son Ares as her lover and then jilting him.

"Excuse me, Mother. Please!" Aphrodite began in a supplicating tone, trying to get her attention. "I know you would prefer to stay angry with me, but I need your advice and help on a family matter." Aphrodite's love affair with

Ares had ended years ago, but she knew that Hera took offenses against her children personally.

Hera gave her a condescending look. "I suppose you mean to talk to me about your son's self-inflicted injury," she said drily. "Believe me, I found out about it only minutes after your father did. I always get the news right after him. I have my agents and they keep me fully informed. But don't worry about keeping the matter a secret. Everybody knows about it now. It's the talk of Mount Olympus."

This was meant to hurt Aphrodite's pride. Hera knew very well that Aphrodite didn't like her family affairs broadcast across the mountaintop. Aphrodite blushed and fought to keep her composure. If she intended to get Hera's help, she dared not quarrel with her. Instead, she played upon a common sentiment, one that couldn't fail to resound in the heart of the goddess of Marriage and Family. "Mother Hera," Aphrodite pleaded anew. "Father won't lift a finger to help, but surely you, a woman and mother as I am, can understand my point of view regarding my son's affairs. I can't get any sympathy from Father. He feels I should let my son continue this idiotic infatuation with that mortal girl. What else could I expect from him? Someone who has debauched so many women, both mortal and immortal?"

Hera gave her a scorching glance. "If you need help from me, you shouldn't remind me of your father's infidelities," she replied. "For once, I see that trouble-making boy of yours getting a dose of his own medicine. His exploits have rocked too many marriages, caused too many people to rush into situations without preparation and commitment. I know that scamp was responsible for the old mayor of Ithaca making a fool of himself over a girl one-third his age. And then, when the old man managed to convince her parents to agree to a marriage, your son deliberately brought a comely young servant into the mayor's household to tempt his young bride. My sources tell me that your son was very amused by the trouble he caused. Why should I, the goddess of Marriage, Home and Family, help him avoid punishment by his own hand?"

"You are too cold-hearted, Mother," Aphrodite retorted, disappointed and angry. "And you have too long a memory."

"I detest people taking marriage lightly, so I opposed that silly old mayor marrying that young chit just as I opposed your father marrying you to the homeliest god on Mount Olympus. In each case, the mismatch makes a mockery of marriage!" Hera declared. "And so, yes, dear. Here's your answer: I could commiserate with you on your unfortunate marriage, but I'm only a mother like you. A mother who watched her son fall for a coquette who used him and then dropped him like an old shoe," replied Hera haughtily. "Even now, my son Ares looks like a sick puppy every time he sees you. Imagine! My son, the god of War, the strongest, proudest god on Olympus, panting over a flirt like you. So, no. I won't help you. Your son can just bear the consequences of his own actions."

Aphrodite stomped her foot in anger. "If that's how you feel about it, I'll find someone else on Mount Olympus who will help me!"

Hera smirked and shook her head, getting perverse pleasure from her stepdaughter's frustration. "I don't think so. Zeus has let his feelings be known. The word is out that he wants no interference. There won't be many who are willing to risk his anger."

Faced with such opposition from her own kind, Aphrodite declared, "If I can't find help on Mount Olympus, I'll find it elsewhere." She was ready to say a curt goodbye when she paused to retort, "Despite my father's dictates, I do have friends. They support me. They haven't deserted me."

"My dear, you are blowing this way out of proportion!" Hera exclaimed with an air of satisfaction, but Aphrodite was not appeased.

"We shall see," she said with great pique. Aphrodite left Hera and walked along the corridor of her father's palace with regal dignity, ignoring the stares of the servants and petitioners but unable to restrain the color rising in her cheeks. In every surreptitious glance, she read the knowledge of her son's misfortune. Shamed, angry and disappointed, she felt lonely in her father's palace, outcast from her peers. Suddenly, she felt she must return to her own villa where her word was still supreme. Only Ares had the temerity to stop her hasty exit.

Ares, the god of War, was a tall, muscular figure with close-cropped black hair and beard. His blue eyes were as hard as the sword that always hung from his belt, and his broad and hairy chest was covered by a breastplate that had resisted the weapons of a thousand battles. Although he feared nothing mortal or immortal, Ares was sensitive to issues he believed might compromise his honor and loyalty. When Hephaestus the Blacksmith in a jealous rage had exposed Ares' love affair with Aphrodite, revealing the couple wantonly making love within the very palace of Zeus, Ares had fled the scene in embarrassment, leaving Aphrodite alone to weather the derision of the other gods. Aphrodite had lost interest in Ares that day, and forevermore after meeting the lover who had come in her dream, the Dream Lover who was the father of her precious Eros, but Ares was always hoping that there would be an honorable way back into her affection.

So now, seeing Aphrodite ready to leave Zeus' palace in a fit of anger, Ares tried to stop her, removing his helmet with a flourish and falling on one knee at her feet. "Madam," he said, "I know you must think that all on Mount Olympus share Zeus' mind, but I assure you that I, for one, do not."

Even in her agitated state, Aphrodite smiled coquettishly at the god of War. "My dear and gallant Ares! How sweet of you to remember our friendship and walk against the winds of public opinion!"

Ares rose to his feet and clasped his helmet to his chest in a heartfelt gesture. "Please let me render whatever service I may toward My Lady. Though I would not raise a finger against our Lord Zeus, I would provide you with subtle help to restore the order of your household."

Since Ares would not compromise his loyalty to Zeus, Aphrodite realized that his promise was a hollow one, but it touched her just the same. "When I told Mother Hera that I still had friends here, I was never more correct. Thank you, dear Ares. Thank you so kindly. I may take you up on that," she commented with a nod and smile before continuing her way.

Ares' words comforted Aphrodite and her color returned. *Father Zeus and Mother Hera,* she thought, *you have freed me to find a solution for myself. Now, my son, you are in my hands. I will bring about your total recovery. And you, you miserable wretched girl, have no allies to defend you from me.*

Chapter Three

The Wedding of Psyche

Medea and Tanna continued to use Psyche's mysterious visitor as a subject for ridicule. Even as months passed, they would never let Psyche forget that evening in the inn. The teasing was all the more cruel because Medea was courted by Proteus, a widowed scholar, and Tanna had the pick of several lusty men. Psyche's predicted marriage to someone – or something – not human added to her sisters' mirth as they themselves moved closer to their wedding days.

For Psyche, conditions were almost unbearable. Before the journey to the oracle, she had known loneliness and discontent. Since then, she had come to know despair and misery as well. She continued to be the adored sweetheart of the village. Her beauty and father's status and popularity made her a regular at every public function. Although she was the object of stares, smiles and comments, there were few who were willing to approach her. She seemed too distant, as much a symbol of reverence as the city colors, a figure of marble whom none chose to study more closely.

The young women her age were pairing off. Even the girls who eluded matrimony could be seen in the company of this man or that. Not Psyche. Never Psyche. She didn't fear a life of solitude. What she did fear was the feeling of lovelessness, the feeling that she would grow old and lose her beauty, never knowing love, never knowing the touch of a hand, the tenderness of a caress, the lingering sweetness of long impassioned kisses. As time passed, what Psyche feared became known to all. Medea and Tanna were delighted to think that she had become untouchable.

Her sisters' torment always had a pattern. They would talk to each other and pretend she wasn't there. They shared stories about their evenings with their lovers. They were only aware of Psyche when they noticed her wounded face and rapt attention. They would then tell her that there was no suitor for her because her good looks had scared them off. Medea pointedly reminded Psyche that beauty was all she had, and that was not enough. Tanna was no kinder. She was quick to make spiteful references to events that she knew were painful to Psyche. The oracle's prophecy and the mishap at the inn never failed to amuse her. She was fond of encouraging Medea, whose wit and malice were particularly stinging.

On many nights, Psyche sobbed into her pillow, fearing that her sisters' words were right. Within a few months, Medea married her old professor, as everyone expected. Shortly after, Tanna married a suitor who had the financial means and nature to satisfy her voluptuous and greedy soul.

When her sisters moved out of the house, Psyche was surprised by her relief. However, at the same time, she missed their company and continued to feel the pain of their rejection and spite. Pericles and Leena, doting parents, couldn't help but see that Psyche was unhappy. On their request, she visited her friends from the village. She attended more parties. She didn't protest when Pericles and Leena busily arranged meetings with strange young men, or had old friends drop by with their unmarried sons. Although young men were eager for her company and didn't protest when their sisters, parents, or friends arranged the introductions, no relationship they formed with Psyche had staying power. One by one, they fell away, as Psyche's parents fretted and her sisters snickered.

On Mount Olympus, Eros struggled with his imprisonment. Never before had his indulgent mother denied him his freedom. Now he was confined to his room and constantly under her supervision.

She hushed his protests by insisting that he was ill. He knew she was right, but he wasn't sure whether it was from his wound or from the discomfort of his forbidden love. For the first time, he was at odds with his mother. The situation had gone beyond talking. Aphrodite had made it clear that discussion was closed. There was no mention of Psyche at all. There were no references to Eros' accident. Nonetheless, Eros understood that he would not be free from his bed until he abandoned all interest in Psyche. He knew his mother would not let him go until she was sure he was cured of his infatuation.

This was no infatuation. Eros knew the power of his arrows and his own susceptibility. All at once, he had no desire for amorous mischief. His thoughts were full of Psyche. Thoughts of her brought both pain and pleasure, and the hunger of desire that had to be satisfied. Although he was sorry that he must disobey his mother whom he loved more than anyone, Eros had decided to give in to the power of his arrow. He had never been in love before. His mother's objections were a challenge which made the game irresistible.

I have powers I've never used, he thought as he lay in bed. *I never had a need to use them, because Mother always let me do what I wanted. I have plenty of time now to test just how powerful I am. If I do this quietly, Mother and her minions might never realize it. I can smile. I can dissemble. I can pretend that I am content to lie here in bed and accept Mother's dictates. I won't be disobeying her; I'll be the very picture of a meek and obedient son. But in reality, my spirit will circle the world, seeking allies in my quest for this forbidden love. I think Grandfather Zeus is on my side. If he agreed with Mother, he would have done something to reverse the effect of my arrow. Regardless of how he feels about it, though, I know he won't help me. He's left it up to me. He's giving me the chance to be a man.*

Eros first took stock of his strengths, those gifts with which he had the most experience and was the most skilled. There was his ability to fly. In distress, he realized he could no longer use this power to advance his ends. Nor could he trust his faithful aim. Although his mother did not have the heart to take away his bow and quiver, they sat abandoned on a dressing table across the room, under the eyes of his mother's servants. He had his invisibility, but that seemed rather useless now.

He must develop other talents, gain experience using those powers that he had not exercised before. Eros remembered the stories his mother had told him about his mysterious father who had visited her in a dream. Although he had never known the Dream Lover who was his father, Eros knew that he had given him awesome and exotic powers. Closing his eyes, under the guise of sleep, Eros concentrated. *I can do more than become invisible,* he thought. *If I have mastery over my corporal self, I can project myself out of my body in spirit. I've done it before, but it was unintentional, instinctive. It's a talent I've never mastered, but one that I need now. If I succeed in overcoming my corporal self, I'll seek allies to help me win Psyche. Afterward, I can seek Mother's forgiveness.*

Deliberately and uncharacteristically, Eros pondered every detail of his plan. He knew he must be considerate of the allies he selected. If their intrigue should be discovered by his mother, she could react vengefully. Those whom he sought for help must be willing and able to take the risk.

Or be beyond the danger of his mother's vengeance, he thought, taken by a sudden inspiration. With resolve, he began to concentrate, calling upon his neglected powers, hoping to complete the first step of his plan. With satisfaction, he felt his spirit rise from his body and float through the ceiling of his mother's villa. From a perch in the clouds, he viewed the countryside and forests below. He then plunged toward earth. First, he saw the tops of the trees, and then he passed through the lacy green and black curtain of their branches. He passed through the multi-colored carpet of meadow flowers and grasses into the deep caverns of the earth. It was here that he stopped, disoriented.

He was deep within a cave filled with dark passageways and heavy air. Below his feet was the rumble of molten lava, churning and rocking the unstable surface. He felt the heart of the world. He was deep within. From a winding passageway, a gigantic and shadowy figure advanced and appeared before him. "Who or what trespasses?" it demanded.

Although he didn't know her well, Eros recognized Gaia immediately. She was immortal, but not related to his family in any way. She had few dealings with Eros' kind and with the humankind that so fascinated the gods of Mount

Olympus. The Ultimate Creator had placed Gaia in the belly of the earth upon its creation and the earth had given birth to her, bequeathing to her the guardianship of every plant and animal, and making her the sole judge as to when humankind's sins against nature would bring about the destruction of the world. The gods of Olympus respected Gaia's age and privacy, and Eros was being bold and maybe even insolent in approaching her now. She was large, dark, and nearly nude. Bristles of short black hair covered her head. A girdle of grass circled her loins but her tremendous breasts were bare.

Mustering his courage and manners, Eros tried to manifest himself to Gaia. He bowed politely. "I am Eros, god of Love, son of Aphrodite and grandson of Zeus. I'm very sorry if I have intruded, but I come desperately seeking a favor."

She remained grim and silent, but finally spoke in a remote voice, "I have knowledge of your conflict with your mother over the mortal girl. What has this to do with me?"

Not discouraged, Eros continued. "I mean to court the mortal, despite my mother's wishes. That's why I have come to you in spirit and not in person. My grandfather Zeus supports me, I know it, and he is head of all Olympus. He has chosen to help neither my mother nor me in this quarrel, but has left me to my own resources. I have friends but I fear exposing them to my mother's wrath if I am discovered. She could find them guilty of disloyalty and punish them. On the other hand, you have many creatures under your dominion. I know many of them quite well and they know me. Ask the birds who it is who waits for their return in the spring and inspires them to make a home. Ask the mammals who it is who makes them yearn for the company of one of their own kind. They'll tell you it is I. I have friends among them who might be willing not to thwart my mother, but to help me build a nest, a den where I can take my mate. You see, unlike my other friends, your creatures are innocent; my mother could not judge or punish them."

A hint of a smile touched Gaia's lips. "You have given this much thought, young man. I'm not totally unmoved by your proposal, nor am I unfamiliar with you and your work. Look here, though. Do you think I should accept a plan that exploits the creatures who are entrusted to me?"

Eros had considered this objection beforehand and had no good answers. He beseeched Gaia: "I don't intend to exploit your charges, and I didn't make this plea with exploitation in mind. I would willingly pay the price you propose if I could think of anything I have that your creatures hold dear. Love is the only thing I own that is of any value to them, and I give that freely."

Gaia could see he was sincere, and his humble admission ingratiated him to her. "I will listen to your proposal," she relented.

Eros continued. "Since my confinement, I have been strengthening my other powers," he said frankly. "I have developed a plan for winning my Psyche and I now have the means to carry it out. I just need the help of a few of your creatures to pose as domestics in a home I intend to set up temporarily in a secret place."

"Temporarily?" asked Gaia with an arched eyebrow.

"Yes, of course," agreed Eros. "After all, my ultimate goal is to gain a wife and be reconciled with my mother. Then I can set up my household on Mount Olympus."

"And how do you intend to set up a temporary household?" questioned Gaia.

"I have learned some amazing skills. I have learned how to leave my body and become spirit, as you see me now. Invisibility was always possible for me, but never before could I be in two places at once, so to speak. I learned how to do that at will, and how to carry my spirit throughout the world. As spirit, I can manifest myself to you, your creatures, or anyone else I wish while concealing myself and my identity from my love under a cloak of invisibility. From my imagination, I can create and inhabit the illusion of a palace so lovely and seeming so real that no mortal could resist it. So while my corporal body remains bedbound, my spirit courts the woman I love. I am hoping that a few of your creatures will join me in my palace and help me win her heart."

"You would naturally accept any petition my creatures put forward as wages?" asked Gaia.

"If it were within my power."

"You would accept that any contract between us is conditional?"

"I would accept on any terms."

"Very well," Gaia replied. "You'll have your answer in a few days."

Eros bowed once again, pleased and gratified. Then he left the region of Gaia and made what he thought might be a pleasant visit to his beloved Psyche. It had been some time since he had last seen her. By the time his spirit reached the house of Pericles, he was tense with anticipation.

He noticed a figure leaning pensively against a window sill on the second floor and passion flooded his senses. Time had not eroded his love for the sad and lonely woman. Invisible to her, more silent than the night, he studied her features. Time had not eroded her beauty. The melancholy eyes that gazed into the moon's brightness likewise glittered and shimmered in its light. How gently the brightness caressed her cheek, the delicate curve from mouth to breast! Her lips were parted and her exposed teeth shone like the pearls in a fine necklace. Her hair was long and silken, shiny and soft, tempting to touch. He moved irresistibly close and smelled the clean fragrance of her skin, fresh from the bath. For a second, he almost forgot himself and reached out a hand to caress her. But no, he couldn't. Although he was invisible to her and in spirit form, she would still experience a touch. The temptation to touch her and to speak to her was struggling with his logic. His arms itched to grab her and carry her away. If he had been merely invisible but in bodily form, the abduction would have been easy to execute. In spirit form, it was impossible. Besides, her screams and resistance to the brutality of this rash approach would not smooth his path to her heart. So he resisted his urges and considered another course.

He looked at Psyche again and more thoughtfully, trying to gauge her feelings. He saw she was even more unhappy than she had been when he had first met her. Looking deeper, he realized that the curse his mother had asked him to inflict upon her was indeed operating as intended. He must delay his plan until he studied Psyche's situation. He returned to his sickbed and his mother's servants wondered at his improvement. The god of Love was indeed responding well to rest and plenty of sleep, they reported to his anxious mother. At this, Aphrodite rushed back to his bedside and was gratified to see Eros smiling brightly at her. In his greeting, there was once again the warmth and confidentiality which had always characterized their relationship and made them so close to one another. Maybe, just maybe, the quarrel between them was coming to an end.

Feeling the strain between himself and his mother ease, Eros was much more comfortable researching Psyche's situation. While his body was in the guise of sleep, his spirit revisited the home of Pericles. He saw that Psyche's malicious sisters returned to the family often, both disenchanted with married life but too dishonest to admit it.

During their visits, they continued to torment Psyche, although they now envied her single status as well as her beauty.

Neither Pericles nor Leena could deny that Medea and Tanna had a point when they said that Psyche's beauty and local fame had made her unmarriageable. It did appear that the young men seemed more repelled than attracted by her standing within the community. Even the young women refrained from offering their friendship to the girl who was the undisputed town beauty. It would have mattered less if Psyche had been content with her loneliness, but of course she was not. The doting parents could see with each passing month that she was becoming more unhappy, that the possibilities of companionship were slipping away from her. They began to ask themselves why their daughter was so unlucky. They began to organize dinner parties in a panic of desperation. They sought the names of eligible bachelors from friends and business associates. They arranged blind dates and "incidental" meetings with acquaintances who happened to have sons. In spite of their energies, the young men fell away one by one. A first date was never followed by another. No one came to call. No one asked for Psyche. It appeared that there would be no love for the youngest daughter of Pericles and Leena.

Throughout this trying period, Pericles kept thinking about the words of the oracle. He concluded that it was somehow his fault that Psyche was so unhappy. The oracle said she would make a magnificent marriage to someone who was not human and he had been simply content to take his daughter home and carry on with life as usual. Maybe he should have carried his pilgrimage further and sought his daughter's mate more aggressively. There was only one thing Pericles could think of to rectify his error. At the end of his resources, he called the family together and announced another pilgrimage to the oracle.

Although a bit annoyed at the inconvenience of such a trip, Medea and Tanna were pleased for a distraction from their routine. Psyche, being the reason for this journey, was much more uncomfortable, and viewed the appointed travel day with dread as she packed her clothes and toiletries.

With satisfaction, Eros had witnessed Pericles' decision. The father of his beloved Psyche had unknowingly smoothed his path by his decision. Moreover, the decision allowed Eros to assume a more aggressive stance, and he much preferred action to inaction.

In his invisible spirit state, he stood with Psyche in her bedroom and watched her prepare for the trip. He saw her move from her closet to the satchel on her bed, simply doing the mundane and ordinary things people do when packing. For Eros though, each movement was seeing Psyche at a different angle, watching the slither of soft curves and muscle under a silky nightgown drawn over her breasts and hips and draping sinuously down her legs, ending at her bare and slender ankles. The aspect of his love's form, scarcely hidden under the fragile cloth, brought forth a wave of passion he could barely control. Enflamed, he found himself moving toward her, fighting a desire to touch her and caress her, even in his spirit form. He was almost touching her. He could smell her scent, see her breasts rise and fall with each breath. He leaned so close to her that the stray hairs from her head would have stirred with each breath he took had he been merely invisible and not in spirit form. He held back his greatest desire, but bent his lips close to her ear and whispered, "Psyche, I love you with all my heart. Come to me and cast aside this loneliness."

His soft words cut through the silence. Startled, Psyche jumped. She looked around the room as though she didn't trust that she was alone. Although Eros was aching to take her in his arms, he moved away from her and repeated the words in a louder voice. He was surprised at his audacity. Suddenly he who had inspired romance in others felt as shy as any youth experiencing first love. His longing and passion burned so fiercely that he was afraid he would consume her. It had been bold to speak his love, but he had hoped it would be enough to convince her of the importance of seeing the oracle. But, as he looked at her, he saw that she was more frightened than inspired. She put her hand to her mouth to stifle a cry and her eyes were bright with terror. Then she ran from the room to seek her parents' company. Eros was suddenly alone. With a melancholy sigh, he considered the difficulty of his love and all its pain. Fervently he whispered, "You must be mine, my darling. It is your destiny."

Feeling strangely fatigued, he returned to the monotony of his sickbed. This time, his sleep wasn't feigned. In the midst of a dream, Eros saw himself walking through a wooded area. He didn't know the place, but he had the impression that it was remote and solitary. Suddenly, through the trees, he saw a clearing, with radiant sunshine bathing a large meadow of wild flowers. As he stepped into the light, he found himself facing four other creatures who came out of the forest to meet him. He quickly recognized Gaia, now human-sized, and then acknowledged the crow, rabbit, and lioness who stood by Gaia's side. The guardian of the earth did not smile, but stood with grand and solemn dignity.

"Let me first admonish you," she said, "by saying that I had second thoughts about your proposal. I sympathize with your feelings, but I have no desire to deceive the goddess of Beauty who has never done me harm and who indeed has aided me in my work. Moreover, I don't take lightly the exploitation of the creatures whom the Creator has entrusted to me. I am certain you are sincere when you say that you will not exploit them and that this arrangement is temporary, but I can't risk their safety.

"That being said, I want you to know that I decided to honor our agreement by setting your proposal before the creatures of the earth. I was surprised by the number who expressed a desire to help you. There were so many that I had to question each one of them to determine their motives and sincerity. After the interviews, I selected the three creatures you see before you. Let me introduce them to you. "

"This rabbit is Lapina. Last month, a dog tore into her warren and killed her children. She volunteered so she could ease her grief. Please respect her loss and her desire to comfort herself in service to others." Eros bowed to the diffident brown rabbit whose sorrowful pink eyes were blinking back tears.

Gaia continued. "Millicent the Crow had her wing broken by some cruel boys who were throwing stones at her. She is recovering, but she is easy prey for her enemies. She hopes she can save her life by helping you until she gains her strength." Eros bowed to the crow and she acknowledged his greeting with a tip of her head, staring at him with shrewd black eyes.

"Leona the lioness lost her mate shortly after they were paired and has been alone ever since, but she insists she has much love to share," said Gaia. Eros and the graceful golden lioness at Gaia's side nodded in greeting, understanding that they had much in common.

"God of Love, please understand that each of these creatures has known suffering. Each of them has a broken heart. They are naturally very vulnerable, so let me warn you again. Even though their motivation in helping you touched me most deeply of all the animals I interviewed, I would not have them exploited. You must once again swear that this contract between us is conditional, to be terminated at the slightest complaint made by any of these three. When it comes to the welfare of my charges, I have the final say."

"It shall be as you say," said Eros solemnly. "I am grateful to you and to these creatures and I swear that I will honor our contract in good faith."

"Excellent," Gaia responded, her stern features softening. "I want to say one more thing in regard to this subject, and then I will speak no more of it. I am jealous for the safety of these creatures. Therefore, I'm giving them the power of human speech, and I'm enlarging the crow and rabbit to human size." Slowly, and by degrees, the crow and rabbit became five feet tall. They blinked their eyes in wonder, stared at each other, and then turned to the lioness, who was no longer so large and threatening. In surprise they uttered exclamations in a new tongue and, despite their sorrows, laughed with delight for the first time. Eros grinned at their comic expressions of amazement, and then recalled the dignified purpose of the meeting. He bowed before the guardian of the Earth. "I am grateful to you, Gaia, and to these three generous creatures. It shall be as you say."

"Now that I have spoken my admonishments, let me give you my guarantee," continued Gaia. "I understand the motives of my charges and promise you their full cooperation, dedication and loyalty during the course of this experiment. And with our combined powers, I assure you that all the natural distrust and animosity which divide our many species shall be dissolved for the course of this contract. There shall be no predator and no prey, but all will live in harmony. To ensure that my lioness will not sicken for want of meat, I shall temporarily suspend her need for it during the course of the contract, so that she may live in fellowship with the rabbit and crow and so that they need not fear her.

You have my word, god of Love, on their faithful service." And with this, she stretched out her hand to Eros.

The youthful god extended his hand in return, thus sealing the contract between them. "I know a secret place, far from city crowds and curious eyes, where your charges will find a quiet, rustic and wooded environment that I believe will be as pleasing to them as to my sweet Psyche. Allow me a few more days to conclude business, and then I shall return to take them to the place I have set aside."

Gaia nodded her head gravely and the vision faded. Eros' eyelids fluttered open and he found himself once again in his sickbed. His mother's servants were exclaiming happily among themselves, noting the look of satisfaction and joy that had come over the youth's sleeping features.

"You slept well, Master?" they asked.

"I had a most pleasant dream," Eros replied amiably. Then he feigned a yawn and adjusted his position in bed, as though he wished to return to his sleep. All further questions and inquiries were stopped, and Eros was relieved. He must be careful not to betray his satisfaction. There was a lot more to be done before he could return to Gaia and conduct her creatures to his secret abode.

Left alone with his strengthening mental powers, he concentrated until his spirit once again lifted above the sick room. It took flight over Mount Olympus and then plummeted toward the villages and farmlands of the mortals below. He followed the route Psyche and her family were taking on their journey to the oracle and arrived there well ahead of them. There were no visitors to interfere with the young god's interview. When the immortals visit, all other appointments are cancelled.

"Oracle!" Eros called, attempting to manifest himself.

The dormant oracle aroused itself quickly, chagrined at its unpreparedness. "My lord Eros," it gurgled, in quite a different tone from that in which it addressed the pilgrims. "How may I serve you?"

"Oracle, I require a favor of you regarding Psyche, the daughter of faithful Pericles," Eros began. "But first, I would like to know what you know of her future and of the circumstances that brought about my visit."

The oracle responded quickly, "I would tell you all that I know, sir, but my own vision is somewhat cloudy. I apologize."

Eros shrugged in mild impatience. "It doesn't matter. Just tell me what you know. Take your time, if it helps. Have you, like all Olympus, knowledge of my recent illness and its cause?"

The oracle considered, and then responded ingratiatingly, "Only hearsay, my lord, which I dared not accept as true. I'm sorry you've been ill and hope that you are feeling better."

"I am mending, thank you. You can assist my recovery marvelously if you can answer my question and perform a small service for me. Once again, tell me what you know of Psyche, the daughter of Pericles."

The oracle responded, "My lord, she sleeps alone, in the room she once occupied with her cruel and unnatural sisters. Her father is a most pious man who is due for another visit. Her mother is a loyal spouse and a loving parent. I see that Psyche's stay under their roof is soon to end. There is a strange and powerful figure in her future. I do not see him clearly, but I believe he is not human. He will come to claim her in a windstorm and will carry her away. Even now, I feel that he is most impatient to have her as his bride."

Solemnly, Eros said, "You have seen clearly, oracle. I am that superhuman figure you are seeing. I am seeking your help in that very purpose."

"With great regret, my lord, I must decline," apologized the oracle. "Believe me, I would do anything – anything! – to help you under other circumstances. Now that you've told me, I know that the gossip is true. But I have already received instructions from my master Apollo. He stands by Zeus' decision not to meddle in a quarrel between you and your mother. I cannot help you, nor can I help your mother thwart your ambitions toward this mortal woman."

Eros was not dismayed. "You cannot assist nor obstruct me, but you must continue your prophecies, mustn't you? I'm sure that Apollo didn't say that you weren't allowed to tell the pilgrims what you know."

"Of course not," responded the oracle. "I think my master only meant that I should not actively support you or your mother."

"Very well," said Eros. "When Pericles and his family come, I want you to tell them that the bridegroom is impatient for his bride, that her parents must relinquish her to him immediately. Tell them to prepare for a marriage on top of the mountain that sits in the shadow of Mount Olympus. Tell them the bridegroom expects a wedding procession that is worthy of the most beautiful woman in the village, and a priest to accompany the wedding party. The marriage must be scheduled two weeks to the day following their visit to you. And, of course, it is vital that you tell them nothing regarding my identity. Let it only suffice that they know that the bridegroom has mighty powers, and the capability to exact terrible revenge if his instructions are not followed."

"I hear and obey, my lord," said the oracle humbly. "The fate of the daughter of Pericles is sealed."

In satisfaction, Eros left the oracle and returned to his bedroom, where he had not been missed. As he lay among the sheets, finer and softer than satin, he quickly noticed the presence of a sweet breeze in the room. He recognized Zephyr, the great South Wind, with whom he had had many collaborations in the past. Eros had seen how her fragrant breezes fanned the spark of love and he had been her willing companion as she circled the world to encourage the coming of spring and the bursting of life from a barren and frozen wasteland. Sensing her now, Eros closed his eyes and addressed the wind in silence. "Zephyr, I feel your presence all around me. Tell me why you have come."

The answer came in a gentle gust. "I have traveled around the world, my lord, and have heard the gossip of the gods. I have passed through the wilderness and have witnessed the mighty spirit of Gaia moving among the earth's creatures. I have come to help you fulfill your heart's desire because you and I have always been allies. You move the heart to love and I provide the atmosphere that makes passions flower. If you wish, I can provide the gust which will transport your bride to her wedding bower."

"Compassionate wind, your assistance is most welcome. I would like you to perform another service for me. Within a week, I will call on you to transport three of Gaia's charges to my honeymoon palace."

"It will be as you say, my lord," breathed the warm sweet breeze. "I stand at your service. Say the word and it will be done."

Silently, Zephyr departed, leaving Eros with his plans complete. Now in truth he could lay back to rest and savor his success. Already, he could feel Psyche in his arms, and he felt stronger, more satisfied than he ever had been. Now, independent of his mother, he had made a way for himself, stretched himself in ways he had never imagined, took pleasure in a man's accomplishment. The mischievous boy had not been left behind; he had merely grown and ripened.

To Psyche's dismay (but not to her surprise), Medea and Tanna joined the family in the journey to the oracle. They were bored and restless and very eager to leave their husbands behind. Her sisters' presence made the uncomfortable trip even more unpleasant. She didn't want to be the subject of the oracle's prophecies, and she didn't want her malicious sisters speculating on her future. She hoped her sisters would forget her experience with the "intruder" that had been the object of so much amusement during the last trip. Of course, when the women were once again sharing a bedroom in a lodge, Tanna reminded Medea of the incident and they both roared with laughter.

"You never heard from him again, did you, Psyche," gloated Medea. "The athletic suitor who climbs walls like a fly and waters his lovers down like rosebushes?"

"Maybe she's hoping to meet him again. The oracle said her husband was not human and everybody knows that no other human or nonhuman has ever asked her for a second date," added Tanna, snickering.

Psyche endured their insults and tittering in silence. Unlike before, she was less wounded by their words. She felt as if she were burdened by something larger and heavier, by a crushing fate toward which she was slowly walking; she was too afraid to be offended by her sisters.

Now the entrance to the oracle was in sight, but far different from before. There were few pilgrims today, and most of the concessions were closed down. Of course, it was not the right season for pilgrimages, but her father, in his earnest piety, could not postpone theirs a month or two. Despite the off-season, the park around the oracle would still have been beautiful, had the day been sunny and clear. Today, however, the clouds sat low and gray in the sky, and the shadows made the afternoon look like evening.

After the valets came to attend to their horses and carriage, Pericles strode dramatically through the gate and threw himself flat before the statue of Apollo, begging for good omens. Psyche came to kneel at his side, looking for blessing and mercy, thinking more of the Creator who remained a mystery than of the handsome stone image in front of her.

The family moved on. Not even Medea was in the mood to sneer. Psyche didn't notice her look of contempt at Apollo's statue. Tanna had always been bored by the interview with the oracle, but today, she looked nervous. Only fateful Leena experienced no shift in mood. The path to the oracle was darker than usual. The family descended the narrow passageway to the mouth of the oracle. The walls of the cavern seemed to be painted with eerie shadows of purple and green.

Pericles approached the oracle trembling, hat in hand. Reverently he began, "Oh oracle, you know that I, your servant, have called upon you during times of family crisis. Pardon my presumption in asking more about the fate of my youngest daughter Psyche, here. Her sisters are married, but she has no suitors, no hopes of marriage. Is she to be a virgin forever, with no husband to warm her bed?"

The oracle steamed and smoked, and the sulfurous odor filled the chamber of the cave. The family drew back, weak-kneed with fright. The green and purple colors became putrefying and cadaverous in the darkness. "I told you before, oh man, that she was to make a marvelous marriage to a husband who is not human," stated the oracle. "Why do you delay the wedding vows? Her husband already waits for her on the top of the mountain that sits in the shadow of Mount Olympus. He will brook no more postponement. He is a most powerful creature, and he is impatient. If you value your safety, you will wait no longer. She must be married within two weeks from now, or all will be doomed."

The oracle fell silent, leaving the family desolate. Pericles and Leena wept and beat their breasts at their daughter's misfortune. Medea and Tanna were amazed and distressed by the oracle's threats, so unexpected and uncharacteristic. Psyche felt numb, lifeless like the statue in Aphrodite's garden.

In the middle of their grief, the oracle boomed out, "Did you hear what I said, man? I said that the girl Psyche must be wed two weeks from now to a powerful super-being who is waiting on the mountaintop. He wants a grand wedding. He wants a procession, with the town's best priest performing the ceremony. He wants lots of guests. After all, this is your daughter's wedding we're talking about."

Pericles staggered to his knees. "Yes, yes. Of course, of course." Then he struggled to his feet, his face as gray as the cavern rock as he led his family back home, his shoulders bent with tragedy and grief.

When they arrived in town, Pericles sorrowfully went to the town council and told them of his daughter's terrible fate. Immediately, a wail went up in the city. The pet, the beauty of the village, was to be the bride of a monster! Some townspeople claimed to be unsurprised by the news. Hadn't it been said that Psyche would never have a mortal husband?

Reluctantly, the family and townspeople prepared for the wedding day. Psyche felt numb and went about the preparations in a trance, trying on a pathetically beautiful wedding dress and ignoring her mother's noisy sobs as alterations were made. Her sisters agreed to accompany her as part of the wedding party, but firmly added they would go no further than the foot of the mountain.

On the day of the wedding, Psyche, her family, and a crowd of wailing celebrants left her father's manor to proceed to the mountain. In her white bridal gown, Psyche felt more like a sacrifice than a bride, a virgin sent to give her blood for the perverse desires of a cruel and false creature. The weeping of her townspeople contributed to her feelings of martyrdom. For this purpose, she had been singled out among the girls of her village. Now she would truly pay for the tribute of her people. She tried not to cry, but to look straight ahead with an air of dignity and calm, so that everyone would always remember her that way after the creature devoured her.

At the foot of the mountain, many of the celebrants fell away, quaking with fear and staring with dread at the long pathway to the top. Their cries of grief and regret were wrenching. A few steps more, and Medea caught Tanna's arm and pulled her back. The sisters stared at Psyche's straight and resolute figure as she continued her procession up the mountain. From this point, friends, well-wishers, and relatives could go no further. They looked in horror at the mountaintop, darkening with mist and clouds, assuming the shade of night, although it was merely afternoon. Bravely, Pericles and Leena continued at their daughter's side, as well as the priest, who was losing his nerve. This trio exchanged frightened glances; Psyche alone kept her pace.

Psyche's feet seemed inches above the rugged path. She hardly touched the ground at all. Ahead, the path twisted through a dense cluster of pine trees and became lost in the shadows. There was nothing but darkness waiting for her. She didn't know when she would ever see light again. Yet she was compelled to go on.

At this point, the priest put up a hand to stop Pericles and Leena. He determined to have the exchange of wedding vows on that spot, many yards from the summit. Seeing the encroaching darkness and fearful of the mysteries ahead, the priest prayed for the indulgence of the terrifying bridegroom so that he might avoid going the rest of the way.

"Young woman, halt your ascent!" directed the priest in a loud voice.

Psyche turned to face him and her parents. Standing a distance in front of them, she was cloaked in shadow except for a ray of light that caressed the curve of her cheek and dissolved into the whiteness of her wedding gown.

"Father and Mother!" cried the priest. "Do you bear witness that this is your daughter?"

"Yes," Pericles and Leena affirmed, clutching each other like frightened children.

"And do you willingly give her to the man who has come to claim her?"

"Oh, I fear we must!" exclaimed Pericles.

The priest looked up the path toward the obscure summit and could discern no manner of creature present to play his part in the ceremony. Nevertheless, he held up his hand and cried out, "Where is he who comes to wed Psyche, the daughter of Pericles and Leena?"

"I am here behind the veil of darkness!" boomed a male voice from out of nowhere, sending a thrill of terror down the spines of the four mortals who heard it. "Speak the ceremony swiftly, priest," it insisted. "I've run out of patience."

"The woman is yours then, presented to you by the consent of her parents and friends," replied the priest, lowering his hand with a flourish to indicate Psyche. "She stands here by her own volition, accepting the yoke of marriage and the bonds of love and faithfulness."

The priest held up his hand again. "You in turn must swear to love and honor her, with all your heart and body," intoned the priest.

"I do swear," replied the voice of the eerie bridegroom.

The priest stretched his arms to include the entire company. "Then, by the power vested in me by the gods of Mount Olympus, I pronounce you man and wife."

At those words, Psyche sought the faces of her stricken and adoring parents. She held out her arms to them across the distance as if she could share one more touch before being torn away.

Although the breeze that was now swirling around them was pleasant, the four mortals on the mountain shivered as it attempted to force them apart. Their hands could not touch. They couldn't cross the void that separated priest and parents from bride and bridegroom. Then the priest hurried Pericles and Leena away, growing more terrified at the insistent breeze that seemed to want to rush Psyche up the mountain. It was strange, beautiful and terrifying at the same time. It was strong, but it was also warm, sultry and fragrant. The priest knew for certain that he was in the presence of immortality. He knew Psyche must make the final climb alone. With tears, she walked the long dark pathway, her eyes bent over her feet as she ascended the slope, her heart in despair. As she drew closer to the mountaintop, the darkness grew and the wind increased until it whipped around her.

She was helpless against it. There was no discomfort as flower petals flew against her skirt, eddies of multi-colored leaves brushed against her face and caught in her hair. Large bright insects with crystal wings and velvety red, blue, green and black bodies circled her head. They and the leaves seemed to whisper eagerly. "She has come! She has come!"

Chapter Four

The Palace of Pleasure

Expecting to be met by the master of these beasts at any second, Psyche shut her eyes, bit her lip and waited in the wind at the top of the mountain. The blackness whirled and hid her face from the people below. Then the ground dropped beneath her feet and she was lifted, carried away by the breeze until she began to fall. It was not a hard and fast fall, but a soft and slow one, like that of a snowflake. Now she opened her eyes and saw herself in a world of indigo blue, blazing with stars the size of apples. Planets, murky or clear, also appeared, watching her in her fall. Meteors, curious and short-lived, streaked by her with tails of gold, lighting the universe brightly, briefly. Then the dark blue sky lightened to the hue of a robin's egg. Now the planets were birds and butterflies, welcoming her with the soft swish of wings against her arms and shoulders as she fell. She could see the treetops in blossom, flowers of all species and color turning

69

their heads in the direction of the sun, a world of perfect splendor and loveliness.

The ground was as soft as a featherbed when she landed. For a few minutes, she cowered on the ground, afraid to stand and confront this unknown world. Then she scrambled to her feet and looked around defensively, as if expecting an ambush.

Instead, she found perfect peace. A quiet glade lay in front of her, lush with greenery and filled with the sighing of the leaves on the trees. Wildflowers sprang with sensual abandon out of a plush carpet of grass. A few feet to the left ran a brook, gurgling music as clear as chimes. The water was so pure she could see to the bottom, where the golden sand was stirred by rainbow-colored fish.

Then she turned and saw a palace of breath-taking beauty and magnitude. How had she missed seeing it before? The large golden gate before the entrance was open and seemed to be beckoning. Slowly, she passed through. The great wooden doors of the palace opened as if they had life, welcoming her to a brightly illuminated interior.

The sight surpassed all dreams of splendor and opulence, but she was just as frightened as curious. This would have to be the home of the beast and this was her destiny. She couldn't retreat. It was her doom either to die or to live here in paradise with a horrible monster. She might as well find out which.

Surely there was nothing to fear from what she saw in the first room she entered. The walls and the floor space were filled with paintings, sculptures and artifacts from nameless people and endless time. The images of harmony, beauty and love were obscure, and yet strangely meaningful, as if communicating with an all-knowing spirit within her. The color and grace of every art object displayed genius and delight.

She heard nothing in the first room, nor in the hallway, which could prepare her for the second room. When she opened the door, a flood of sound startled and then delighted her. On every side were instruments suspended in mid-air, each in animation. There were players, but they were almost transparent. They seemed engrossed in nothing but their music. Indeed, after being in the room for several minutes, she herself could think of nothing else.

Nevertheless, curiosity pulled her away and through passages which led to gardens and fountains and balconies. At the center of the palace was a large courtyard in which trees, grass, and flowers grew around a pool. Along the edges of the pool were couches, chairs and tables, intended for entertaining or meditation. Walking along one of the cobblestone pathways that cut through the yard, she realized the palace had been built around several acres of the most beautiful meadowland she had ever seen. So large was this park (she couldn't possibly consider it a courtyard now), that Psyche saw squirrels, rabbits and birds nesting and caring for their young.

She returned to the palace to continue her tour. The library contained shelves of books, leather-bound collections of the most passionate love literature of the centuries. In another room were patterns of wild jungle colors with fragrant green foliage. Each room was lovely, with its own charm and surprise. Sometimes there were bright bowls of fruit and goblets of wine, or small tables bearing food. She knew the food had been prepared for her, but she wouldn't eat or drink anything. Much of the fruit was unknown to her and she didn't trust the prepared dishes and wine. She suspected they might be poisoned.

She heard voices coming from another hallway. She followed the sound and was amazed to see a very large rabbit and crow, and a majestic lioness engaged in housekeeping.

Pamela Jean Horter-Moore

They were a charming trio of animals, pleasantly chatting with each other, like the laundry women in Psyche's own village.

Work stopped, however, when they noticed her presence. They came forward to greet her, solicitous and welcoming.

"My dear, we are so happy you could come," the Rabbit said. "We've been expecting you."

How strange it was to look a rabbit in the face! It was as tall as she. Its eyes were gentle and kind. The Crow was nearly as tall; the black satin feathers on her wings were closely folded over her back, as if she had only recently recovered from injury. The lioness was lovely, graceful and golden, with soulful eyes and a solemn expression.

"You can speak!" Psyche exclaimed.

"Of course we can," replied the Crow. "How could we serve you well otherwise?"

"But how can this be? What is this place? Why am I here?" asked Psyche.

The Rabbit chuckled maternally. "So many questions! You'll know the answers in time."

"Yes, it's best not to be impatient," added the Crow.

"But I've got to know!" Psyche insisted. "What is to become of me? Am I to be eaten by a monster?"

All three of them laughed. "No, my dear," said the Lioness quietly.

"Where am I?" asked Psyche.

"Questions again," said the Crow with a sigh.

"My dear, we cannot answer your questions," said the Lioness. "That's the truth. You must learn your own answers."

"Then, may I ask what you are doing here?" asked Psyche.

72

"We can answer that," said the Rabbit. "We are here to serve you, my dear. This is your home now."

Psyche looked around her, amazed.

The Crow cut short any further questions. "Friends, we must allow Psyche to become accustomed to her new home. She might be tired and hungry. All of these other things can wait until later."

Psyche would have protested, but it was evident she would get no further with the trio. Indeed, now that she had recovered from the shock, she found herself somewhat fearful of her housekeepers. The jaws and claws of the lioness would have inspired terror in anyone, but the sight of a human-sized rabbit and crow was hardly less frightening. If she hadn't overheard their friendly words to one another, she would have fainted away the minute they were aware of her presence. Their intentions toward her seemed to be kind, however, so she allowed herself to be escorted to her room. Along the way, the trio gave her reassurances, saying that the master was delighted that she had finally come and that she was sure to be happy in her new home. Psyche said nothing, but noted their enthusiasm. They seemed to be privy to a delightful game in which she was one of the players. If so, she was at a disadvantage, because she didn't know the rules.

Psyche's room was lovelier than she ever could have imagined. It was decorated with the colors of a seashell. The bed was like an open oyster piled high with soft pink silk and linen cushions. The walls were pearl, translucent rose and bronze, with a rainbow tint of green and purple. Seaside plants flourished around the room.

They bathed Psyche in a pool as large as her bed and just as pink and translucent in appearance. The dear creatures ministered to her, putting the fragrances that were the untampered scents of a thousand gardens into the bath water.

Then they dressed her in a white gown, light as a spider's web, which clung to her body and fell into the curves of her breasts and hips. They let her hair loose and bound her waist with a ribbon as pale as moonlight. Within the glow of the bathhouse walls, she could see herself and knew that she had never been more beautiful. Was there more in the treatments of her attendants than mere pharmacists could concoct? She looked almost, no, just like a goddess. It was no accident.

Intuitively, she knew that the Rabbit, Lioness and Crow were expecting someone else. Someone who wanted to see her. Someone who was undoubtedly responsible for this wonderful palace and its unusual attendants. When she inquired, the Lioness answered, "The Master returns tonight."

A chill ran through Psyche. "When do you expect him?" she asked.

"My dear, we do not presume to expect the Master. He is very busy. He comes and goes as he pleases."

"And his name?" Psyche prompted.

The Rabbit shook her head. "We do not presume to give you information about the Master."

"He is the reason you have bathed me and dressed me, isn't he?" Psyche pressed, growing more uneasy. "This in effect is to be my wedding night."

The animals didn't answer her. It occurred to her that they just might not know. Thus did they put Psyche aside. She spent twilight in speculation, her sense of wonder deadened by her sense of dread. When her loneliness pressed her, she sought the company of one of the animals. She would say nothing but would watch them in their work. It was marvelous to see a rabbit sweeping or a lioness carrying water to the kitchen. None of them spoke much to her. They were part of the grand conspiracy of which their master was the head.

Psyche's fear was at its peak in the early hours of evening. But as the hour approached midnight, she felt relief in the continued absence of her host. Maybe he had lost interest. Maybe he had forgotten that she was his guest. Maybe something had interrupted or changed his plans. Feeling a little better, Psyche approached each of the animals for information regarding her master. In each case, the animal was taciturn, deflecting her questions with comments that encouraged no discussion. The Crow paused from her work to declare, "I'm sure I don't know, girl. You must ask the Master yourself." The Lioness replied gently, "You know I can't tell you, so why must you ask?" The Rabbit said, "There is no use worrying about it. The Master isn't going to bite you, my dear. Do you think any of us would stay a minute if we thought he was going to hurt you?" There was small joy in the Rabbit's logical remark. The master must be horrible indeed if the three animals who served him weren't even willing to talk about him!

Finally, Psyche stretched and yawned and indicated she was ready for bed. She turned to walk alone toward her bedroom when she was stopped by a rustle of feathers and the feel of talons laid gently on her shoulder. "No, my dear. That's the wrong direction," said the Crow, as if speaking to a child. "Your bedroom is to the left, up the staircase, and down the hall. That staircase to your right leads to another wing of the palace. You must never, never go there. It is restricted to the staff." The other animals were soon by her side and, once again, they were escorting her to her bedroom. *They are hiding something from me,* Psyche thought. *They might not know a lot, but they know more than I. What are they anyway? If they are the animals they appear to be, how did the Rabbit and Crow become so large? Why do they have human speech and why do they have the ability to perform human chores? It seems that these talents have come upon them only recently. They don't seem to be completely at ease with humans. They are really very awkward at dissembling. Even a child could do it better. Even a child could think up lies that were more convincing.*

Psyche was pleased to know that she could still come up with such an observation, especially considering her distress. But the information was useless, like discovering a piece to a puzzle and realizing that it adds nothing to the solution. *Oh well,* she thought. *If I am fortunate, I will live to pursue these questions further with these single-minded creatures. If I am not so fortunate, I will be relieved of my captivity by death.* Reflecting on her thoughts, Psyche thought they were very noble and brave, but false. She really did want to live, even if she were the prisoner of a monster.

For that reason, she welcomed her host's delay. She welcomed the animals' goodnight wishes and felt relieved when the door of her bedroom was closed. She bolted it tightly and smiled in grim satisfaction. She moved pieces of furniture in front of the door and then retreated to her bed, feeling small comfort. She drew the bed curtain around her, sank into the fluffy bedding, and fell into a light sleep.

She was awakened by a light knock on the door. She was dumb, made mute by apprehension and by the unlikely hope that whoever it was would go away if she didn't answer. After a silence, she expected to hear the knocks repeated. Instead, a presence filled the room like incense, powerful and impossible to ignore. It pulled back the bed curtain in a single movement. It was invisible, and yet compelling and pleasurable, like a draught of a most potent and prized red wine. At the same time, Psyche was stricken with terror, confronted by a supernatural intruder whose incredible powers made doors and walls no defense, who possessed the advantage of stealth and who had apparently pushed aside all her obstacles with no effort at all.

A gentle tenor voice addressed her unspoken fear. "Don't be alarmed, Psyche. It is only I, the one who loves you."

Suddenly, she was no longer afraid. The presence before her was so benign that fear seemed unthinkable. "You ... you love me?" she asked, breathing hard.

"Alas, yes!" sighed the intruder. "I've done terrible things for the pleasure of this moment, but not so bad that I regret your being here. Be patient with me, Psyche. There are things I cannot tell you. I cannot reveal myself to you. I must ask that you follow the rules of the house. In return, I will love you as no woman has ever been loved. Your happiness will be my pleasure. Can you bear these burdens?"

A spark of uncertainty moved Psyche. She felt a net closing over her, her apprehension rekindled. Instead of answering his question, she asked, "Who are you? Are you the one to whom I was led?"

"Yes. It was I who brought you here. It was I who was your groom on the top of the mountain."

Psyche caught her breath. "You are the one about whom the oracle spoke?"

Once again, the voice admitted, "Yes, I am the one. Psyche, my love, forgive my haste in bringing you here. I must confess, I've been a cad. I'm usually not in favor of kidnapping someone in order to win her love."

"Who are you, or what are you?" asked Psyche. "You speak sweetly to me and yet you don't show yourself." She wanted to add that she was afraid, and yet she didn't want to admit it.

His heart full, Eros said, "Don't you remember the times I've come to you in this form? Don't you recall the journey home from the oracle several years ago, when I appeared outside your window at the inn and touched you in your sleep? Don't you remember my words to you as you packed your clothes for the last journey to the oracle?"

Psyche remembered and began to tremble. So, her senses had not deceived her. Those strange experiences that had made her so frightened and that had made her the object of her sisters' ridicule were mysteriously joined with the fantastic prophecies of the oracle. "Yes, I do remember," she replied in a frightened voice. "It's all making sense now. You are the inhuman thing about whom the oracle spoke. It is you who forced me to leave my home and enter into marriage in order to avoid your wrath. What manner of being are you, and why are you hiding yourself from me?"

The voice of Eros drew a sigh of frustration and longing. "You are full of accusations, and I don't blame you for being angry and frightened. After all, your behavior is all too human. Once again, I ask forgiveness for my impetuousness. Yet, I know if you understood what I understand, you would be patient with me. If I have acted rashly, ruthlessly, it was only due to the circumstances under which I have been forced to operate. You might think that I have tremendous power over you and this household and you might be impressed with the means by which I have brought you here, but if I were really powerful, I would have done it differently. I would have courted you most sweetly and would have won your heart like an honest man. Instead, I have made great effort and have taken great risk to bring you here and to provide all the comforts that might help me win your love. You fear me because my invisibility and power give me advantage over you, and yet, my love, it isn't true. I have done a terrible thing; I have been disobedient and dishonest to the one who loves me most. All for the love of you, Psyche. All of this has been for the love of you."

Touched, Psyche replied, "I don't know who you are or what you are, but I am willing to give you the benefit of the doubt. If your character is like your words, I believe we might yet reach an understanding. I've got to warn you, though; I don't know how long I can be patient. I won't promise not to ask questions. Very soon, I think I should want to know why I am being held here and who is holding me."

She concedes and then she confronts me, thought Eros. *This sounds more as if she were conducting business than making love. She shows me that she will not be my slave. This is a new Psyche I am seeing now, different from the one who let her sisters hurt her. I like her. But how shall I answer her? Should I show her more power? Should I persuade? No. Instead, I'll be cool and rational. I'll show her that I can be reasonable.*

"I understand," answered the soft voice. "That is as much as I might expect right now. Will you suffer my visiting with you a while longer, my love?"

With each word, the intruder gained Psyche's favor. She smiled. "Of course." She made another gesture of concession. "After all, if I am to understand correctly, you are my husband, are you not?"

"Yes, and with all my heart," answered Eros.

Shyly, her face turned aside, Psyche murmured, "Some might say that your being my husband gives you power over me; that I could not refuse you even if I wished."

The velvet voice dropped lower as it replied, "Some might say that, but that is not my way. I might be your husband, but I am also a stranger to you. I can afford to give you some time. I am not one of these men who would barge unwanted into a woman's sanctuary, although I suppose I should not speak too soon when I say that." Eros glanced at the pile of furniture in front of the door, his self-reproach giving way to amusement.

"Of course not," Psyche returned, her face solemn, not comprehending the irony.

"You tried to keep me away," said the voice.

Psyche nodded. "I was afraid."

"Are you still afraid?"

For a second, Psyche was tempted to lie, but instead nodded her head and averted her eyes from the direction of that haunting voice.

With a sigh, the voice spoke. "I should not be surprised that you are afraid. I am invisible to you. I have kidnapped you, taken you from your family and kept you here. You are served by three incredible animals. I shouldn't wonder that you are terrified. You must know, however, that you are no stranger to me. You are the novice in this love affair, and I am the one who has boiled alone in this passion. My passion and compassion struggle with each other, but my nature tells me which of the two will triumph. This courtship and honeymoon can't last long; you and I are in considerable danger. I, too, can't say how long I can be patient."

As the voice spoke, it conveyed a sense of urgency. The gentle and yet insistent words assailed the defenses of Psyche's virginal modesty. All her life, she had been the object of admiration and devotion, but no one before had addressed her as a woman and a lover. She was overwhelmed by the magnitude of his emotion. Despite her husband's invisibility, she experienced his desire and knew it was a struggle for him not to touch her, to hold her, to make her yield to a lover's caress. She was moved in a way she had never felt before and she was nearly as frightened by what she was feeling as by the persona of the individual in her room.

He spoke again. His voice was above her and farther from her now. "I must leave you now, my love," he said. "If I stay longer, the wound you have given me will bleed afresh. Think of it, Psyche. Think of how I am pained for love of you. Think of how I have struggled to provide you with the most lovely wedding bower a woman ever had. Think of how you have longed for love all your life, Psyche. It is here. Think of me kindly while I am away. I shall come to you again tomorrow."

There seemed to be a second of hesitation, as if her intruder had some unfinished business. Then, suddenly, the voice and the presence were gone.

Alone again, Psyche found herself breathing hard, amazed and dazzled. She hardly knew what to think. Never before had she heard a lover's voice. Now it had come to her in a torrent of passion, ardent and persuasive. The admiration of her villagers seemed bloodless now and insincere by comparison. The sacrifice she was being asked to make now was more dear than the tiresome smiles that she had been forced to wear while being exhibited by the townspeople. She, the ice princess, was under a heat so strong she could not help but feel its fire. She was desired.

This, she thought, *is the adventure of my life. This is the type of thing that happens to women of legend. But how am I cast? Am I a captive, a heroine, or a lover? And who or what is it that comes to me? If I could judge by voice and manner only, I would say that he seems pleasant and eager to please. On the other hand, he lured me here and has made me a captive in this luxurious prison. Why? What does he want from me? How can I trust someone who won't reveal himself to me? He is inhuman. There is no denying that. No human could have his powers. But what? Is he so horrible that he can't reveal himself?*

A parade of fantastic monsters passed through Psyche's imagination. She saw giants and cyclops, trolls, demons and gremlins. She saw specters of walking corpses and twisted bodies. She saw dragons and manticores, and monsters of every variety and shape.

She recoiled at the images her mind conjured up, even as she tried to rationalize that the silky voice and gentle manner of the intruder were out of character for the monsters she imagined. She extinguished the light and returned to bed, but sleep didn't come quickly.

Eros was as drained and exhausted as she was alert and uneasy. His spirit moved away from Psyche's door and sought the company of the three beastly servants. They were waiting for him in the kitchen, gathered most curiously around the table, sharing their observations concerning their mistress' state of mind and the likelihood of this experiment's success. Each eye asked the same question of Eros, but none of the three was bold enough to state it. Their acute senses told them how fatigued he was. The meeting with Psyche, the maintenance of the illusion of the Palace of Pleasure, and his manifestations in spirit had strained him. Nevertheless, he talked with them, thanking them for their help and describing his conversation with Psyche. Yes, he was satisfied with this first meeting; it was too soon to expect her love and trust. He then excused himself and moved toward the staircase to the right of the main room, the one Psyche had been told not to use. He passed along the long hallway to the bedroom which he had made for himself in an obscure part of the palace. It was a simple room containing only a bed and a window overlooking the courtyard. This was the center of the Palace of Pleasure, this mirage he had concocted from his own spirit. Only here could his spirit rest to build up strength to continue the illusion. But here little could be feigned. Although he was the god of Love during his wakeful hours, and capable of the most wondrous powers, he was as vulnerable as he could ever be when sleeping. So his spiritual self slept in the simple little room created from his imagination. His real person remained in his bed at his mother's villa, maintaining the appearance of illness and sleep before the eyes of the jealous goddess Aphrodite and her most loyal attendants. He was living at two different levels, deceiving both of the women whom he treasured more than anything else. How long could he last? How long would it be before he could unite the two portions of his life?

When he opened his eyes and found himself in his bed at the top of Mount Olympus, when he saw his mother's beautiful face looking down upon him with such devotion, he longed to stop the charade. He wanted to sit up in bed, take her hands in his, and share his experiences with her. He wanted to show her that his love and suffering had made him a man, a man who was not afraid to pursue what he wanted.

Chapter Five

Love Without A Face

When Psyche awakened the next morning, she thought she must have dreamed the visit by the gentle-speaking invisible stranger. She saw the furniture still propped up against the door, undisturbed, and she began to doubt the reality of what she had experienced. She could not, however, doubt that she was here in this fantastic room surrounded by colors as translucent as the sea and objects of beauty so rare and wonderful that a queen might envy them. She rose from the bed and marveled that she had spent the night in what appeared to be a sea shell, sleeping on bed linen that was so fine even her father had not seen its like on any merchant ship from the Orient. Curiously, like a sleeper in a dream, she slowly walked around the room, lifting and studying this object and that, opening drawers to find web-thin lingerie and wardrobes filled with silky pastel garments. She took one of these and wrapped it around her. She then placed a pair of golden sandals on her feet. Never had clothing felt so light, so airy and free. She twirled joyously around the room, seeing her reflection on the glossy walls. Once again, she was startled by her own beauty. Accustomed as she was to seeing her face in the glass at home, she was amazed to find that this palace agreed with her, that her beauty was more wondrous here.

It was curious that she was even more beautiful here, was it not? It was just one of the things that seemed too unworldly to comprehend. And when she thought too much, she quickly remembered the strangeness of her plight and the reality of her imprisonment. No invisible lover could assuage the gnawing doubt at the back of her mind. It lowered her spirits, and she became considerably more subdued as she opened the door a crack and peered down the empty hall leading to the staircase. Seeing no one around made her brave. She tip-toed down the hall and reached the top of the staircase. Directly below, the Rabbit was dusting. She seemed to be expecting Psyche; her twitching nose was pointed in her direction and her eyes were on her before Psyche was even aware of her presence. Psyche was startled, but hid her discomfort, even as she descended the stairs.

"Good morning, my dear," said the Rabbit.

"Good morning," Psyche replied, smiling in spite of herself at the idea of exchanging pleasantries with a rabbit.

"And how did you sleep?" asked the Rabbit. Her tone suggested more than mere politeness.

"Very well, thank you," Psyche responded. The Rabbit stared at her in silence, evidently wanting to say more but not knowing how to say it. She seemed to be even more curious about Psyche than Psyche was of her.

"I suppose you must be hungry," said the Rabbit.

Psyche had not considered food at all. Now she found that she was indeed hungry. She smiled shyly and nodded.

Given a mission, the Rabbit abandoned her feather duster and led the way to the kitchen. Psyche found it was difficult to walk with a creature that hopped. The animal talked continuously.

"Crow is making seedcake for breakfast," she rambled. "That's not entirely surprising, do you think? I'm a vegetarian, myself, so that suits me just fine. We share kitchen duties, we three, so of course each of us wants to prepare her specialty when it is her turn to cook. I'm preparing a salad for lunch. I hope you like greens."

Psyche assured her that she did.

"It's not that you couldn't have any food you wanted, just for the asking," the Rabbit elaborated. "The Master is so powerful that I believe he can arrange anything. But it helps to be accommodating, don't you think? One can't be asking for special favors all the time."

At the mention of the master, Psyche's questions began to bubble up in her mind. She was disappointed when they reached the kitchen far too soon, and the conversation took a different turn.

The air in the kitchen was warm and fragrant with the smell of newly baked seedcake. Indeed, as they entered the room, they happened to see the Crow taking the last batch from the oven. Furiously, she flapped her uninjured wing to keep her balance while carrying the cakes to the table. Potholders guarded her talons from the heat of the pan. It was a sight that made Psyche wonder why the master's visit should strike her as more strange than what she had encountered from these curious creatures.

Relieved of her burden, the Crow invited the Rabbit and Psyche to take some of the cakes already cooling on a plate. The three of them were enjoying breakfast when the Lioness walked in. She declined the cakes, saying she had already breakfasted. Psyche wondered what the carnivore found to eat.

There was a brief silence during the meal. Feeling more mellow because of these very domestic surroundings, Psyche tried to reintroduce the subject of the master. When she did, she noticed that each animal's face became guarded. Unaccustomed to and unable to cope with human-like emotions, they didn't have the sophistication to cover their feelings.

"Who is he?" she asked.

"We can't tell you that," answered the Rabbit quickly.

"What is he then?" she pursued.

"We can't tell you," the Crow repeated.

"Is he human?"

"Do you think he is?" asked the Crow.

Psyche considered. "I don't know. His voice seems human enough, but I've heard few human voices so gentle and pleasant. He's invisible. That is a power beyond human ability, and yet not so fantastic. Miracles more wondrous than that happen every day, even in the human world."

The animals marveled at her faith and were pleased that she had so quickly accepted the lover whom they called Master. They were surprised that this hurdle had been so quickly overcome, for they had previously understood that human hearts could be more stubborn than that. For the rest of the afternoon, they applied themselves merrily to their chores, certain that their stay in this arrangement would end soon and would end successfully. At the same time, they regretted that the challenge had been so easily met. The Lioness especially missed the challenge of the hunt and the pursuit.

In this benign frame of mind, Psyche welcomed her invisible guest that evening and for the next few evenings. With each visit, she learned more about his exquisite tastes in art and music, his love for romantic literature. Her heart fluttered when he quoted passages from love poetry still yet to be written. Although new to her ears, these verses contained sentiments in common with the love poetry of her day. How was it that he seemed to know how to answer her questions of love but couldn't reply to the simplest question of all: Who are you?

She continued to ask, thinking that by her very persistence she might pry an answer from him. Each time she did, he would respond, "Psyche my love, I can't tell you now. Please accept that there are good reasons for my not telling you. Have faith in me. Just know that I have come with no other purpose but to love you."

To love me? Psyche felt her heart throb, although she wasn't sure whether it was from dread or excitement. Here for the first time was a lover who was bold enough to go to her and claim her, and yet he could not reveal himself to her. His feelings for her, however, were no mystery. With every visit, he became more ardent. At the end of the second visit, he kissed her hand; she could feel his lips lightly brush her fingers. By the fourth visit, he was kissing the inside of her wrist with a passion that both startled and excited her.

Her sister Tanna had told her about passion. She had told her tales of surrender in boastful and mocking tones, reminding Psyche that both her heart and her bed were empty and lonely places. She spoke of the clinging kisses, the groping hands, ever straying to the limits, ever eager to trespass. She spoke of insistent words, wheedling, begging, threatening, flattering, while flesh was flushed and damp with lust and breath was rapid. The lover became the enemy, laying her resistance to siege, calling for her surrender.

Psyche had shuddered when Tanna told her of such things, and was less sorry for her own loneliness. Now, the invisible one had shown her that love-making didn't have to be like that at all. Even though he expressed his desire and love for her most keenly, he didn't attack her. No, his approach was subtle; so subtle that she had to remind herself the outcome in either case was the same – her surrender. He was like a stranger who brings his family into a foreign land and wins the affection of the natives through his friendliness, affability and willingness to assimilate. Only later do the natives discover his purpose, but then his family has prospered and has grown powerful, and he has no obstacles to his ambition.

There was a significant difference, however, between their relationship and that of other lovers; she was already his prisoner. She had been in his power long before he had claimed his love and had begun his pursuit. This place, this marvelous place with its strange and timeless treasures, its kindly talking beasts, was her prison. Her lack of knowledge was her torment. If he loved her, why did he imprison her? Why didn't he set her free?

Her doubts become small in his presence. He was so gentle, so solicitous of her. Even in her most restless times, she had to admit that her lightest request was honored. But the questions that mattered the most to her, those that made sense of all this confusion, were deflected with sighs and vague words of regret. Strangely enough, she never thought to ask him for her freedom. His feeling for her was so strong and his actions since her abduction had been so tender that she was powerfully drawn to him and intrigued by him.

By day, he was gone, and, with him, the madness and passion of her adventure. She wandered through the palace, pausing for a few minutes to gaze in wonder at this timeless treasure or that. How could any mortal amass such a collection of objects? Here was one of her favorites: a crystal globe in which a strange city of light and mortar lay, and, when shaken, produced a swirl of snow over a strange and miniature landscape. With each new discovery, she came to view the world as a grouping of little worlds, each layered on top of another, each living in every time simultaneously. Each person, too, was at once unique and alike, living several lives in one, living the life of everyone. *What a queer notion,* thought Psyche. And yet it didn't seem much more queer than her existence here at the Palace of Pleasure, under the hospitality of her invisible captor-husband.

By day, the animals busied themselves around the palace, doing all the human things that they had always thought would be fun to do, serving Psyche in all her needs, as they had pledged they would. Of course it was unnatural that a lioness might take up gardening, that a rabbit might enjoy housework, or that a crow might develop a talent for cooking, but to them it seemed completely normal. They were simple creatures who just lived as well as they could. They didn't worry about what was natural or unnatural. The reality of their agreement with Eros, solemnly witnessed by Gaia, negated the unreality of their human powers, and they thought nothing more of it. It was true that their changes first evoked strange and startled laughter, but now the Rabbit and Crow had no fear of the Lioness. She, for her part, had no desire to harm them. Within a few days, she had lost her desire for meat and was able to join the herbivores in a meal of salad and seedcake.

Of greater concern to them was the welfare of Psyche and Eros. They had sensed a shift in Psyche's mood since that first morning when they were so certain this would soon end with her capitulation. They watched her as she meandered around the palace. The Lioness observed that she had the look of a caged cat just awakening from the sedative of her captors. There was the surprise and relief of not having been injured and the empty pleasure at the richness of her cage. There was also the vacant look of despair the powerless wear when they realize they have no freedom. To the Rabbit, Psyche had the look of one who has seen a furtive shadow creep into her warren, violating her sanctuary and craving her blood. The Crow observed that Psyche's condition was much like her own: a struggle for wholeness and flight. The animals knew that, even in her happiest times, Psyche wanted to know the answers to her questions. Efforts to engage her attention were short-lived; the animals' ridiculous and touching attempt to distract her with a human board game was not enough to keep her seated for an hour.

At night, when Psyche retired, the animals shared their speculations about the mind of their captive mistress.

"At first she seemed happy here," remarked the Rabbit. "Remember how we all marveled at how well she seemed to be taking this? I guess we were premature."

"The human heart appears to be just as complex as we had heard it was," said the Crow pensively.

"But not more complex than the heart of the superhuman," replied the Lioness, thinking of Eros.

The Lioness was justified in her concern. Eros' resolve, resources, and strength were taxed as his physical being remained in bed at his mother's villa and his spiritual being struggled to play the roles of palace, master, and lover. The exhausted figure in bed at Mount Olympus was the one of these that was not an illusion, who slept so often and yet seemed so restless that Aphrodite was considering taking the matter up with her father and stepmother again. If she had been an ordinary, human mother, she might have been fearful for her child's life, but Aphrodite didn't have a mortal mother's care. Eros' long sleep was beginning to concern her, but she considered that this rest might be what he needed to purge the girl Psyche from his heart.

She was not aware of how her son was suffering for love. He was suffering, not only for love of Psyche, but also because he loved his mother Aphrodite too and didn't want to defy her or hurt her. As he carried the burden of his charade, he thought there was no one but the faithful animals who knew the extent of his pain. But, of course, there were other eyes to see. Mighty eyes that measured him, that saw him tested for the first time, that were compassionate but maintained a disinterested distance. There was no mischief now in the youthful god's bearing. Instead, he held rigidly to his course and pursued Psyche as seriously as a hunter pursues the most magnificent deer in the forest.

Every night gave meaning to his actions, as he went to her bedside and courted her, testing her wit and her heart. His invisibility added to the intrigue and he saw that she was as fascinated with it as she was impatient. He couldn't tell her that he couldn't be seen with her, that he had to come to her invisible as a spirit even as he had been invisible himself when he had first seen her at the lodge with her sisters. One look at him in his visible spirit form and she would know right away who he was, and not only she, but Aphrodite herself. His mother would then see through his disguise and know that he, sleeping in her villa, was covering for his spirit and its manifestation as the Palace of Pleasure. Eros must be content at this point to court Psyche slowly, to play at his invisibility as if it were a new game, to gratify her fantasies and yet to keep her here, as well entertained as possible.

After several nights of brief conversation, he came to Psyche's bedside, as was his practice, and found her not huddled defensively in bed, but waiting for him by the table. When he greeted her, she picked up a glass of wine, filled it, and handed it to him. He took it from her and whispered his thanks as her eyes marveled at the sight of the glass in mid-air.

"I thought I should offer a gesture of graciousness in return for your generosity," explained Psyche stiffly.

"It is you who is generous," Eros replied, more warmly but no less seriously than she.

Psyche turned her face from him. Carefully, she said, "In my culture, there are husbands who beat their wives and treat them cruelly. There is no one in my village who wouldn't envy me now. There is no one who would say that I haven't made a great marriage. You've been kind to me, and I don't want to be ungrateful, but I don't think we've reached an understanding on some very important matters."

Eros silently came up behind her and boldly put his hands on her shoulders. "It is true that there are things that I haven't told you. Believe me when I say that it is not from dishonesty that I hide these things from you, but from danger."

"Danger?" she repeated, turning her head slightly toward him, but not, he noticed, pulling away from him.

"Yes. Danger for us both. I remain invisible for our own safety. Please don't be frightened when I tell you that to know me could very well cost you your life."

"My life?" she cried out, shaken. "How can that be? What have I done to deserve such treatment? I'm innocent of anything that could cost me my life."

She was standing up now, facing him, very, very close. Eros regretted his words but once again she let him take her by the shoulders and whisper in her ear, "My dear, you have made a powerful enemy."

She shook her head, incredulous. "But how can that be? I've done nothing wrong."

His grip tightened on her with urgency as he bent once again to whisper in her ear. "You have caused great offense.

You could never find absolution for all your offenses. I am here to save you, but for a price."

"A price?" she repeated dully.

"Yes, the price of your freedom and maidenhood. The price of a marriage to a faceless stranger."

"It is the price many women in my culture pay," replied Psyche with bitterness.

"Except that I, too, am paying a price. I have stepped between you and the danger. I have...built...this Palace of Pleasure, and have brought together everything to protect you from harm."

"But what is my offense?" Psyche asked. "I've done nothing wrong."

Gently, Eros contradicted her. "Yes, you have. I can't explain it all to you, but think. Think of your greatest burden and then imagine yourself as your greatest enemy. What is it in you that you hate? That is where your offense lies."

At first, his words seemed foolish, but the longer Psyche thought about them, the truer they seemed to be. Although she wasn't quite sure she knew the answer, she felt remorse for her many small and countless sins, and her eyes began to overflow with tears. "I have sinned!" she declared. "I have given offense every day of my life, in countless ways. Most of all, I feel ungrateful. Ungrateful for who I am and what I have been given."

He was so pleased by her sudden insight that he wanted to join her in her tears, but instead he touched her hair and smoothed it from her face with a tender hand. She looked straight through him in his invisible form and then closed her eyes, and he knew she took pleasure and comfort in his touch. His fingers brushed her face and she seemed to turn to him, not resisting when his arms tightened around her and he gently, shyly, touched her lips with his. They were soft and yielding. They were sweet and eager. It seemed to both of them that the past was but a prelude to this moment. Even to the god of Love, this love was new, as if no one else had ever loved before. For her, it was as if her icy heart had melted. This was the only thing she had ever known of desire and passion.

They remained embraced, suspended in time. Psyche shut her eyes and forgot that she must appear to be clasping the empty air. Finally she broke away and crumbled to the floor, crying afresh. He was startled by her turn of behavior, but emboldened by their new intimacy. He crouched by her side and cradled her in his arms. "My love! Why are you weeping?" he beseeched her.

"I don't know who you are," she said. "This palace, these talking animals, they are wonderful. It is all very beautiful, but so very strange. I was alone before, but my life was simple. You have taken me away from all that. You have complicated my life. And now... now I think I've fallen in love with you. What is to become of me? Who are you? What do you want?"

Eros didn't want to hear anything else after she had spoken that triumphant sentence. At last he thought he had the prize within his grasp. He felt like a man, a conqueror, a hero. (She had said, "I've fallen in love with you!") But her forlorn questions reminded him that his work was far from over. How could he reply? He thought, *I do not know what will become of you, my love, nor of me. I don't know how long I can continue this charade. I'm so tired, and I know Mother is getting worried. What will happen if she discovers me? Can I protect Psyche or myself from her wrath?*

To Psyche he said, "I can't tell you who I am, but I can tell you what I want. I want to be your love, Psyche. I have given you mine, with all my heart. I want your faith, Psyche. There are things I cannot tell you and that you can't possibly understand."

"Where do you go, then?" she asked. "After you leave here?"

"I look after my household, naturally," replied Eros. "I talk with the housekeepers to see whether there is anything that requires my attention."

"And after?" Psyche persisted. "Where do you go after you speak to them? When I am here in this room, alone, where are you? Are you alone too?"

Her words were like another thrust of the arrow. "Yes," he answered sadly. "I am alone too. When I am away from you, I get no relief. I must be attending business, or sleeping to regain my strength."

Psyche was unsatisfied. She said carefully, "If we are truly married, we should not be alone. We should not have secrets from each other. I know our worlds are far apart. What do we have in common? This palace, these beasts, your invisibility. It's all too fantastic! I come from a world of merchants, farmers, laborers, and politicians. We see your world in glimpses. We pay homage to it and then we forget about it. Ghosts, nymphs, monsters, and ... and invisible people, they're the subjects of stories and rumor."

"You have seen that my world is not all stories and rumor. You fear it because you don't know it. How could you possibly? Don't turn from me simply because I have powers you cannot understand. Don't be angry at me because I cannot tell you the answers to everything you want to know. You and I are both prisoners. I am in love with you and I am paying dearly for it. Let that suffice for now. One day I swear I will tell you everything. On that day only will we be truly married. We will have no more reasons to hide."

Eros stopped, considering the effect of his words on Psyche. He had never been so brusque. Had he gone too far? No, he could see that she appreciated his honesty. Her eyes were cast down modestly. She was inexperienced with the passion she had seen him demonstrate. She said, "You once told me that it was you whom I married before I was carried away from the mountaintop to this place. If that is so, you know that my parents gave me away to you, as they had been instructed by the oracle. You need not sleep alone at night. Your rightful place is beside me."

She could not see him shake his head. "The right to sleep beside you is yours to give, not your parents' nor the oracle's. As long as there are secrets between us, you will sleep here and I will sleep in the southern wing of the palace, alone and apart. Only my servants, the Rabbit, the Crow and the Lioness, know how forlorn and barren the rooms in that wing must be!"

She thought he must be speaking of that portion of the palace denied to her. Something in her invisible lover's words made her pity him and long to comfort him. She said tenderly, "I hope, then, that the day will come soon when there will be no secrets between us."

Gratified, Eros turned and took Psyche in his arms. He slid his hand behind her head and bent her so their lips met in a passionate kiss. She felt herself crushed against a lithe body, as slender and muscled as an archer's. The skin that touched hers was softer and smoother than the garments she wore. She wished she could see the color of hair that felt like silk between her fingers. Caught up in kisses that seemed endless, she put aside battling thoughts and took pleasure in the flesh invisible beneath her fingers, in the caresses and kisses she couldn't see.

In the morning, she was alone again, but still warm with the glow of his love. She took her time dressing, thinking in satisfaction that she, like her sisters, now knew what it was like to be touched. Like Tanna, she had felt the heat of a man's passion. Tanna had been wrong in one sense: it was not a beastlike hunger that seeks only to pleasure itself, a mechanical act that ceases when satisfied. Instead, it was an act of giving, an act of sharing with another person a marvelous journey that leads to a pinnacle of joy and completion.

She came down the stairs singing, startling the Lioness, who carried a basket of tomatoes in her powerful jaws. Psyche offered to take the basket from her, still rather uncomfortable in the company of any lion, even a vegetarian. She picked a tomato from the basket and looked at it with wonder. "It's beautiful. What is it? I've never seen it before. Can you eat it?"

The Lioness was again surprised by Psyche's buoyancy. Was it typical for a human to change moods so quickly? "I understand that you can," the Lioness replied. "I know little about it, being a meat-eater until now. I've never seen anything like it. But then, the Master is not an ordinary man. I suppose his knowledge of these things goes beyond yours and mine. Take heart from his wisdom and consistency, and from his passion for you."

"Then, all of this is a mystery to you too?" Psyche asked.

"There are many mysteries," said the Lioness. "I think I know why I am here. That is enough for me right now."

"Why are you here, then?" persisted Psyche.

"To serve you and the Master," replied the Lioness.

That was not a new answer, and it did not satisfy Psyche. "How did you come into his service?" she asked.

"I saw that he was kind and generous. I could see that he was burning with desire for his mate. I too was burning with desire for my mate, but my mate was dead. I wanted to help someone achieve what I had lost."

"Oh, I'm so sorry!" Psyche cried out in compassion, throwing her arms around the soft velvet neck of the Lioness. All at once, she saw the Lioness as not merely a lion, but a living being; a living being who had chosen the constraints of service as a means to heal her broken heart. So these animals were not merely servants of an invisible, yet clearly powerful, being. They (or at least the Lioness) had volunteered for their positions. Moreover, the Lioness' account portrayed Psyche's invisible lover in a most favorable light. Psyche was stirred by the reference to herself as a mate.

"It's quite all right, thank you," returned the Lioness cordially, turning the conversation delicately away from herself. "I am quite happy to stay here as long as I am needed."

"And how long is that, do you suppose?" Psyche inquired eagerly, disengaging herself from the embrace, pleased that she had managed to get answers to so many questions at once.

"I don't know," replied the Lioness. "The Master himself is the best judge of that."

"I have something to do with this, don't I?" asked Psyche. "I have the feeling that something is expected of me. I've told him time and time again that he and I are married. In the place I come from, he already has complete liberty with me. And yet, he doesn't take it."

"Would you want him to?" asked the Crow, flying haltingly in from her housekeeping task in the forbidden southern wing and catching the last of the conversation. She looked as though she might perch on the Lioness' shoulder, but suddenly remembering that she was five feet tall, she settled to her feet directly in front of Psyche.

"No, I wouldn't," Psyche replied. "I've heard terrible things about the way some men treat their wives. The act of love is something savage for them. But he is not like that at all. He is so gentle and patient with me."

"He is in love, and you are the fortunate one whom he has chosen," said the Rabbit, who also had dropped her housework to join the conversation.

"Then you know him well?" pressed Psyche.

"Well enough, and less than we'd like," replied the Lioness.

"I hear more questions coming, and, as usual, we have no replies," admonished the Crow. "You must learn for yourself the nature of your lover's heart. Why do you seek hearsay and opinion when he himself visits you nightly?"

"My people are not accustomed to this," Psyche said, spreading her arms to include the entire palace.

"This is not your proper habitat?" inquired the Rabbit, surprised. "We had always understood that humankind, like rabbits, preferred to live in a warm, enclosed structure like this."

"That is not what she means," the Crow drily corrected the Rabbit. She turned to Psyche. "Are you trying to tell me, my dear, that the kings of your people don't build structures like this, or that no wealthy man collects objects of beauty simply for the pleasure of having them? Why do you doubt merely because you have met such a wonder face-to-face?"

"Because I am held captive here and I want to know why," replied Psyche.

"But you **know** why!" countered the Rabbit. "It's because he loves you and he wants to give you a chance to love him in return. Let me assure you, my dear, that you are fortunate in love."

The conversation with the beasts gave Psyche a thrill of anticipation as she waited that night for her invisible lover. When his soft voice and presence appeared, she stepped forward eagerly, and he took her hands in his. "Sweet Psyche," he said, "You have something on your mind and in your heart. I can see it shining in your eyes. Tell me your feelings, my love."

"I talked with the animals today, and they spoke very highly of you," Psyche said. "They assure me that you are someone whom I can love and trust."

"I have dear and loyal servants," replied Eros, gratified. "May they be blessed for taking my part!"

"I would like to trust you," Psyche continued. "You have been sweet, but you haven't been honest. If you love me as you say you do, you would respect me enough to confide in me. I would rather you were forthright and told me the unpleasant truth than have me live in ignorance. You have provided me with beautiful surroundings, but you have denied me my freedom and my dignity. Am I a prisoner here? If so, it is sweet captivity, but captivity all the same."

"Sweet captivity! That's an apt phrase which pertains to both of us, my love. I, too, am a prisoner," said the tenor voice. "I am a prisoner of love for you that is so passionate I have willingly chained myself to this masquerade of invisibility. I understand well how frustrating it must be for your questions to go unanswered, but I hope it won't be long before I can tell you everything and show you who I am."

"Then, can you tell me for whom you are masquerading? Is this all for my sake? Or is it for the sake of another?" asked Psyche.

The voice sighed. "For you **and** for another. That is the nature of my misfortune. How can I explain my position to you? It's just a matter of time before I am discovered. Then the masquerade will be over."

"What am I to do until then? How can I be content not knowing what is to become of me?" Psyche asked.

"No one knows," answered Eros sadly. "I could release you, I suppose, but then I would assure your doom. For reasons you cannot possibly understand, you are destined to two fates. One is to live here in my Palace of Pleasure, under the care of my faithful servants and my own devotion. The other fate is doom, a loveless and gray future that grows more forlorn as your beauty fades with age."

As Psyche heard these words, her eyes began to fill. Then the formless arms of Eros came around her and pulled her gently to him. She shuddered with grief and let the hot tears fall on what she could only guess was his shoulder.

"Psyche my love. Please don't weep. Our unhappiness cannot last forever. It's difficult, I know, but I am driven with love and desire for you. I can't turn back now. I'm wounded by love for you. You can't imagine what I'm risking to love you."

"Then, shall I know you only by night? Shall I never see you nor have your company by day?"

Once again, the forlorn sigh. "No, not now. I dare not see you by day. I'm sorry, Psyche. Can't you love me as I am? Don't you remember the conversations we've had and the sweet times we've shared?"

At these words, spoken with a grief so like her own, Psyche's compassionate heart stopped her own sorrow and she embraced her invisible lover to offer her own comfort. He accepted her kiss willingly, although his old wound gave him pain and his spirit was melancholy. He held her close and wondered whether one always suffered such pain for love. Her long fluid hair, the soft roundness of her breasts close to him, the timid supplication of her body, stirred him with delight, so that the pain was worth the pleasure.

She forgot her fears in his embrace. The reality of his arms, the feel and smell of his body, fresh and fragrant, dispelled her misgivings. His tender words wound their way into her heart. That entire evening, they talked of love and other beautiful things. He would say nothing about himself, but sought her opinions with a grace and interest that she had never heard from other suitors. She watched as a bottle of wine was raised and poured into two goblets. She accepted hers and then stared in wonder as his glass was raised and slowly emptied. Then he would speak and shatter her reflections, reaching her heart as well as her mind.

She felt his lips on her throat. They moved down her neck and his silken hair fell on her bosom. His hands caressed her shoulders and explored the bare skin under her garment. His mouth was once again on hers. She wrapped her arms around him and felt the lean body of the youthful archer. And yet, his skin was softer than hers in texture, just as his hair felt finer and softer to the touch. Suddenly, she wanted more of that sweetness, and welcomed his hands on her breasts. His lips tore from hers and sought her body. His hands caressed her, arousing for the first time in her the heat of a lover's passion.

This was the moment she wanted to surrender. She felt his manliness against her and wanted to make him part of her, to conquer him as he was conquering her. She wrapped herself around him and felt him enter her, with pain and then the most glorious of pleasure. She held him fast and now he was her prisoner, entwined with her, joined to her. And so it was natural and beautiful when they both cried out, came together, and then clung together, spent, neither one nor the other losing, equals in the field of love.

Eros and Psyche enjoyed the night together, but when Psyche woke the next morning, he was gone. She looked at the bed, where her invisible lover had lain. It bore the imprint of no body. She thought the night just might have been a dream, but it was only the natural climax of what had begun since she had arrived in the Palace of Pleasure. She could see no logic in these events. Instead, she experienced a euphoria that had her ghost-walking around the palace by day and early to her bath and bedroom by night. The animals were moved and amused by her behavior. This, they believed, was the honeymoon, that dizzying period where every action is judged in the light of love's fruition.

Psyche spent all day waiting for her husband. After her supper and bath, she carefully selected her wardrobe for the evening. Then in expectation, she sat in the center of her bed until his sweet presence passed through her closed door. In an instant, she sprang from the bed and opened her arms, faithfully expecting him to take her into his. As they kissed, they forgot that they were beings of two different natures, strangers who could love but who could never really be together.

As they lay together in her bed, she felt content to lie against what she thought was his shoulder, and stroke his body. She could not see his person, but her fingers touched warm and smooth flesh. At times, it was easier for her to close her eyes. Her reason could not accept what was happening to her. It was unreal, and yet it was real. Reason retreated before this fantasy.

Reflecting upon these things, Psyche disturbed her reverie to ask, "Darling, I have fallen in love with you and yet I have never known you other than invisible. I assume that you have another shape and form that might be visible to me. Can you tell me more about it?"

Eros could have told her without vanity or falsehood that he was the most beautiful young man she had ever seen, but he answered instead, "What more can appearance tell you about me? The essence of who I am is not contained in my body, but in my spirit."

This enigmatic answer disturbed her, but lightly. He was so gentle and kind to her that it was easy to acknowledge the truth of his words and content herself with the beauty of his spirit.

Pamela Jean Horter-Moore

That is, for a time, Psyche was content. She loved the company of her lover in the evening. By day, her surroundings were elegant and the creatures kind. Eventually, however, she began to miss human companionship. As she lay in Eros' arms, she asked whether she might return home for a visit.

She sensed her husband's disappointment. Then his resignation. "I suppose I should have expected that you would want to return. I find it curious, my love, that you have never asked me that before. You asked me many times why I was holding you here, but you never just asked whether you could go home."

His voice was so plaintive that she put out her hand to touch what she thought might be his arm. "I will come back to you, my love," she said. "I will not be able to be long from my heart."

He sighed in relief. "I should not be surprised by your request," he said. "Even my people long for others of their own kind. It is natural that you should want to spend time in the familiar surroundings of your childhood. Very well. You can begin your visit when you choose. My agents will conduct you to your home."

"And how might I return to you?" asked Psyche, gratified that he seemed so accommodating.

"You may return to me when you wish simply by walking up the mountain where we were wed. Otherwise, my agents shall come to you at the end of two weeks." Eros felt cold fear as he spoke. Suppose Psyche's love faded while she was away from him. Suppose she never returned.

From the sickbed in his mother's villa, Eros summoned the wind Zephyr to carry his love back home. Sensing Eros' grief, the warm wind and gentle breeze shrank away in fear and Eros could not coax her to come. Instead, Zephyr fled

106

Mount Olympus, distraught, and sought the company of her brother Boreas.

Boreas the North Wind was circling the colder climates of the world, settling snow and ice on the inhabitants who live in the land of the fjords and the vast tundra where winter brings frigid nights that last well into daytime. He was shocked to see his sister in his domain, her warm breath frosty from the cold. When she explained Eros' situation and his request, he was willing to help. He had few dealings with the god of Love, their natures were so different, but he was anxious to do him a favor. With characteristic brusqueness, he blew into Mount Olympus to offer his services. Aphrodite's servants exclaimed and cursed at Boreas for his rudeness, but he brushed them aside with a mighty puff of wind and entered the bedroom of their mistress' son. Although they felt the cold of his intrusion, they could neither hear nor see him as he bent to the young god's ear and offered his help.

Eros said, "It is good of you to offer, North Wind, but I was thinking of gentler transportation for my lady."

"But I am available and willing, Master," Boreas reminded him, "While my sister, seeing your disappointment, has fled in dismay and refuses to help."

"Very well, and I thank you with all my heart," Eros replied. "Send a message to my friend the Rabbit and ask her to dress Psyche warmly for the trip."

Psyche packed the next day. She had little that she needed for the visit, but she was careful to select clothing from her new home that would draw curiosity from her merchant father and admiration from her family and the townspeople. On the Rabbit's instruction, she had placed a heavy cloak loosely around her shoulders. Then, for the first time in what seemed to be a long time, she and her three beastly companions left the Palace of Pleasure.

As they walked away, Psyche looked around and tried to recall how this place had looked on the first day of her arrival. When she caught sight of a retreating unicorn, startled out of hiding, she recalled the strangeness and the wonder of her sojourn in the palace. She could hardly believe she was walking away from it now with no hindrance from the master of the place.

Occasionally, she or her companions would turn and watch the palace fade far off in the background as they walked purposefully past fields and glades that were quite similar to those around her village. "What is this place we are going to?" Psyche asked her animal friends.

"We don't know," they replied, so directly that she knew they were telling the truth. "It is enough for us that we are following the instructions of someone we trust."

The further they walked from the Palace of Pleasure, the more unpleasant the weather became. Psyche clutched her cloak closer to her. "Why has it become so cold?" she asked.

"Because your transportation is here," the Rabbit replied.

Hardly had she spoken when the impatient North Wind scooped Psyche up from the ground. Waving hands, paws, and talons in farewell and making promises of return, Psyche and the trio of beasts hastily said their good-byes. As she buried her head in the folds of her cloak to keep warm, Psyche reflected that this journey was not as sweet as her last. There was a sudden rush that took Psyche's breath away, and she found herself standing in front of the gate of her father's home.

Chapter Six

The Homecoming

When Psyche looked at her parents' home and the familiar surroundings of her village, she quickly forgot how tedious it had been to live here with no sense of purpose other than the shallow admiration of others. She was overjoyed when her mother came bouncing from the house in greeting, happier than she could ever remember her being. They embraced, and Psyche reflected that her own joy was deeper since her stay in the Palace of Pleasure. Did love have the power to color the world in an entirely new and different way?

Her mother held her at arms-length and looked her over. What she saw pleased. "My dear, you look wonderful!" she exclaimed in delight. "How are you?"

"Wonderful, Mother," Psyche assured her, and was surprised that her enthusiasm came so easily.

"Dear child, when we sent you up that mountain, we were convinced we would never see you again."

"And I thought I would never see you again. But I'm home, Mother. Home at last."

Leena's eyes went dim, once again reminding Psyche of her capacity for doubt and sorrow. "But for how long, Psyche? How long will you stay with us this time?"

Psyche replied, "No more than two weeks, Mother." She recalled the lover she left behind and felt no fear or dread of returning to him. This was her vacation, as fleeting as her father's trips to the oracle.

Leena had more questions, but instead, she clasped her daughter around the shoulder and led her back to the house. She was thankful the maid had already left and that her husband was still attending business in town. "Here, sit down." She offered Psyche the guest chair and ran to fetch wine. Then she sat down next to her daughter and cupped a full goblet in her hands, as she asked, "How goes it with you, my girl?"

Psyche discovered that she was pleased to talk about the elegance of her new home. She saw her mother's eyes open wide with wonder as she described the highlights of the Palace of Pleasure and of her wonderful and extensive wardrobe. She found she could say little about her beastly servants; it was one thing to talk about the richness of her home and quite another to describe otherworldly marvels. They might think her mad. Her mother was impressed enough to know that she had servants who were at her call both night and day, and who did not ask for time off. There was even less Psyche could say about her husband, the Master. As far as her mother was concerned, it was enough for Psyche to report that he was away most of the time, but very good to her when he was home.

When Psyche's tale was over, she in turn asked about her family and the townspeople. There was little to report, Leena shrugged, much more interested in her youngest daughter's exploits. "Wait until your father gets home," she said.

It was a couple of hours before her father would return, so Psyche couldn't resist meeting him at his shop. Once on the streets, she discovered she was shy of the townspeople. After the quiet of the Palace of Pleasure, their noisy outcries intimidated her.

"It's Psyche!" cried the first of those who recognized her. "It's the queen of our city, returned alive!"

She gave him and his friends a gracious smile as she passed, but she heard their footsteps behind, following her as she moved along the street, shouting out her name for everyone to hear. Before long, a crowd gathered, pushing her along to her father's shop, distracting her with questions.

News of her arrival having preceded her, Psyche saw her father striding out of his shop to meet her before she was within 100 feet of it. Psyche could see that her father relished the crowd around her, as well as the group of admirers that was quickly growing around him as he took command of the main street of the village.

Psyche was crushed by his enthusiastic embrace and found herself mercifully protected by his presence as he led the way back to his home. He brushed aside questions regarding his daughter's welfare, indicating that Psyche would be available for an interview after she had rested with the family. Once again, Psyche recalled why the admiration of the town had been so hard for her to bear. For the first time in her life, however, she found it simply tiresome, rather than overwhelming.

When Psyche sat at the dinner table with her parents, her mother urged her to tell her father about her life in the Palace of Pleasure. Her father, even more so than her mother, was more impressed with the richness of Psyche's new home than with the suitability of her husband. It was enough for him that his daughter was living lavishly and well.

After explaining her circumstances to her father's satisfaction, Psyche looked forward to a quiet evening at home. She was disappointed by the noisy arrival of her sisters.

Once again, Psyche rehearsed the story of her stay in the Palace of Pleasure. Now, she was beginning to gain some familiarity with this version of the events that had occurred following her marriage.

She was relieved when her sisters appeared to be satisfied with her story and turned the conversation to other matters. She forgot to be on the defensive. In fact, Medea and Tanna seemed to be very kind, and paid Psyche a deference that she found surprising. She was touched by this display of sisterly affection and, for once, did not feel left out of their secrets. Was it because she was now also a married woman and unavailable? Was it because her sisters had missed her during her absence? She was grateful, therefore, when her sisters' last remarks to her during the evening included an invitation for lunch at Medea's the very next day.

Her parents went to bed with happy hearts. Although they were still very uncomfortable with the circumstances of their daughter's wedding, her return and her radiant health and happiness gave them confidence. Pericles in particular took comfort in the prophecies of the oracle. "It's to be a great marriage," he assured his wife. "Don't you remember the words of the oracle?" The success of the evening provided them with double satisfaction, for they supposed the rivalry between the sisters was over.

The next morning, Psyche was presented before the mayor and the townspeople. They accepted the story that she was married to an enigmatic being who kept a magnificent villa in the country, and were too polite and superstitious to pursue the matter further. Her reticence and lack of knowledge concerning the identity and business of her husband left the gossips with a lean story and added to her reputation as an empty-headed beauty. The opulence and splendor of her wardrobe proved that she was living well, even beyond the means of her father, but her answers to their questions were so vague that they dismissed her as utterly witless.

For her part, Psyche sighed in relief when the interview was over and looked forward with less fear to the celebration dinner to be held in her honor a few days later. It was easy to compose a glad-to-be-back-home speech. She was merry as her father escorted her from the mayor's office to her sister's house. He dismissed his friends and followers as he passed through the village square and entered the residential section. The lunch appointment was family only.

A servant answered the door of Medea's villa and informed Psyche and Pericles that the professor was at the university and unavailable, but that Medea, the mistress of the house, was looking forward to entertaining her sisters. Tanna had already arrived, the servant explained. As for Psyche's escort home, Medea would see that she was safely delivered, so Pericles need not make a return trip to fetch her.

Pericles thanked the servant with a generous tip, gave Psyche an affectionate bow, and went whistling on his way. Psyche felt vulnerable without him; her sisters still intimidated her. The confidence of last evening's visit had faded with the effects of the wine.

The servant led the way to the laboratory. Upon entering, Psyche had a familiar feeling. Medea was at her test tubes while Tanna sat in an overstuffed chair in the corner, her plump feet raised on an ottoman, a goblet of wine in her hand and a pitcher sitting on the table at her elbow.

Her painted mouth was open with mirth and she was obviously in the middle of a tale of gossip when she spied her sister Psyche.

"Well, there is the little princess herself," said Tanna in greeting.

Medea stepped away from the table and peered thoughtfully at a steaming beaker of chemicals. She gave the servant a piercing glance. "Clean up this mess," she ordered. "And don't you dare disturb that beaker!" Of another servant, she demanded a basin, soap and cloth. Only after she had washed and wiped her hands did she speak to her sister, and then, her greeting was warm.

Taking her by the hands, Medea said, "Psyche, you poor darling. What an ordeal you've been through!"

"Yes," Tanna piped up. "And how brave of you to put on a good face in front of the folks!"

Psyche was touched by her sisters' affection, but was puzzled. "I don't understand," she said.

Medea stopped further talk and motioned to Tanna. "I believe it's time for lunch," she said. "We have much to discuss."

Psyche followed her sisters out of the laboratory and toward the dining quarters. She had always considered her sister's home a dark and spartan place, with only the artifacts of science and scholarship ornamenting the rooms. Once in the dining room, Medea made her servants the unusual request that they serve all courses at once and leave the sisters in absolute privacy. When the last servant withdrew and closed the doors behind him, Psyche had a strange feeling of abandonment and confusion. Her sisters eyed her greedily.

Tanna remarked, "You know, Psyche, Medea and I never thought we'd see you alive again. Now you've come home to tell us about your captivity and escape. Surely nobody has ever had such a horrible experience."

"And we want to commend you on the courageous way you're dealing with it," added Medea.

"I can assure you, sisters, that it hasn't been as bad as all that," replied Psyche, surprised by their reaction.

"Come now," insisted Medea. "You don't have to pretend to us. We understand that you wouldn't want to upset our parents by telling them just how hard it's been."

"Surely, those tales of servants, beautiful artifacts, and wondrous clothing were empty ruses to ease our parents' minds," said Tanna.

"No, they were true," Psyche rejoined. "You were there last night when I showed Father those exquisite gowns from my trousseau, weren't you" Have you ever seen anything like them?"

"They were wondrous indeed," Medea agreed. "They told me just how dearly your captivity was purchased. Your captor has made a monumental effort to win your acquiescence."

Psyche shook her head. "No, it was not like that. They were gifts of love. That's what he told me."

"Naturally he told you that," answered Tanna. "What a fool you are, Psyche. Don't you know that men will say anything to get their way? Was imprisonment with him so pleasant? Did you find him so attractive that your wits were completely addled?"

"Well, truthfully, he's away on business so much that we don't spend much time together. And when we are together, he is so charming and gentle that I believe his words are true."

As both sisters heard Psyche's undeclared statement of love, they stewed with envy and bitterness. Both of them thought how nice it would be if their own husbands were away on business more often. Both of them heard Psyche's elaborate descriptions of the Palace of Pleasure and knew by the candor in her eyes that she was now very rich indeed. Still, they both sensed there was something left unsaid.

"He must have been charming indeed to have won the heart of the village's ice princess," snickered Tanna. "And yet, Psyche, you have never described him to us."

At these words, Psyche hesitated, for she now sensed herself on dangerous ground. "Well, of course he is very handsome."

"Is he dark or fair? Short or tall?" urged Tanna.

Psyche replied "Well, I suppose most would think him neither fair nor dark, nor tall nor short."

The knowing glance between Medea and Tanna was so swift that Psyche didn't catch it. Medea chuckled. "Please pardon us, Psyche, if Tanna and I are curious about the man who won the prize of the village."

Tanna again demanded a description of the Palace of Pleasure, calling upon Psyche to repeat much of the conversation from the evening before. In the absence of her parents, she and Medea could interrupt the narrative with question after question, expressing admiration and wonder at Psyche's answers. Although the smiles were still on their faces, both sisters showed by meaningful gestures that they were envious of their sister's wealth and unable to find any reason to doubt her sincerity, unless she were mad or hallucinating. "How did this wealth come about?" they wondered aloud. Psyche grew uncomfortable and admitted that she didn't know.

"Not know the nature of your husband's business!" exclaimed Medea in amazement. "Psyche, are you a child, that your husband holds such matters from you?"

Psyche felt very foolish. "I know he has business. Every day he leaves me to attend to it, but he doesn't tell me what it is."

"Strange business, I'd say," sniffed Tanna. "You don't suspect it's something illegal, do you?"

Psyche shrugged and stared at her plate.

"Then things are even worse with you than we feared," Medea declared. "You have no control over the situation, have you? You're entirely at the mercy of this husband of yours, aren't you? Not only are you a captive in his golden cage, but you are kept in a state of ignorance. This man you are living with could be a highwayman, a murderer, an assassin who has made his fortune in blood and is hiding away from the company of decent people."

"No!" Psyche exclaimed. "I know little about him, but I know that's not true. Deep down inside, he is a decent man, and he loves me completely."

"Well, as your elder sister, I'm concerned," Medea stated. "I was grieved by the tragedy of your situation before, but now I am desperate to confront this husband of yours and know his intentions."

"Sister, it is not what you think!" Psyche exclaimed. "I promise you, he is good to me. He has promised to tell me everything in good time."

"Promised?" chortled Tanna. "Since when should a woman depend upon a man's promises?"

The sisters were upset, that was apparent. They wanted to know everything about her husband. It was their right to be upset, they declared, because they were motivated by sisterly love. Most of the questions were unanswerable. Psyche herself had asked those questions of her mysterious husband. She found herself on the defensive with her sisters, and very soon in over her head.

"Do you know that you've contradicted yourself several times?" Medea finally asked, with a particularly nasty smile.

Psyche was struck dumb, cowering under her exposure. In misery, she listened as Medea cataloged her slips in logic.

"The truth of the matter is, you don't know anything about your husband, do you?" sneered Tanna. "You don't even know what he looks like!"

"Psyche, I can't believe that you'd lie to us," said Medea. "You've never done that before. Why would you do that to us and to Mother and Father? What are you trying to hide from us?"

Shame-faced, Psyche told her sisters the truth. Throughout most of her story, they sat open-mouthed, listening with amazement while inwardly pleased with the knowledge of her imperfect and horrible love. Scorn hid behind their feigned words of sympathy. "Poor Psyche! She is being held captive by an invisible man. Or, more likely, a monster!"

Yet, their satisfaction was not complete. Psyche was surrounded by elegance, living an existence that excited envy in both sisters. Furthermore, Medea and Tanna were now well-experienced with marriage, and they had reason to wish that their husbands likewise would become invisible.

A silence thick with resentment and insincerity was broken by Medea's sudden question, "What could be the nature of an invisible man?"

"Certainly not like any man I've ever seen!" chuckled Tanna. "And I would think that I have the most experience in these matters."

"Then you believe that it is most unusual?" asked Medea.

"I'd call it rare," replied Tanna.

"But if there were an invisible man, what would be his nature?" repeated Medea. "Would you think him mortal?"

Tanna shrugged. "He could be mortal or immortal. You are the most learned of us, sister. You could expound upon this in the highest metaphysical terms. For my part, I'm a pragmatist. I recall the words of the oracle, and I can't help but think that its predictions have come true."

As Tanna was verbalizing these thoughts, a new vision of her husband filled Psyche's mind, and she was seized by a greater fear than she had ever experienced in the Palace of Pleasure. Her fate was in the hands of an immortal creature with the power to snatch her from her home and then return her. She was the plaything of a supernatural being whose strength appeared to be limitless. His servants were beasts who belonged in the fierce and natural world and who were behaving most unnaturally. With each sister's remark of horror and dismay, Psyche felt increased revulsion for her state of affairs and wished with all her might that she might throw off her captivity. As joyful as she had been with her life in the Palace of Pleasure and her love for her invisible husband, she was now filled with outrage and sorrow.

"Has your invisible husband told you that he has another form?" asked Medea.

Psyche indicated her assent, which caused Tanna to remark, "If he prefers to show himself to you in invisible form rather than in natural form, he must be terrible indeed!"

"Yes," Medea agreed. "He must be a monster, so hideous that he would cause a mortal to faint on sight. Recall all the creatures of mythology. Think of all the incredible beings that fools like Father and his ilk believe in."

"Height must be nothing to this monster," observed Tanna. "Remember how he clung like a fly to the wall of the lodge in which we were staying in order to whisper to his lady love?"

Psyche couldn't help but blush as she recalled how her sisters had ridiculed her at the inn.

"You're right, sister. From what we know of this creature, he must be quite different from us and hideously ugly. If he has beasts for servants, he himself must be a supernatural beast. Perhaps a fly, as you have suggested, Tanna. Have you ever looked at a fly, Psyche? I mean, really looked at one?"

The bulbous eyes and grotesque mandibles of the fly filled Psyche's imagination to the point of nausea, and she continued to shiver as she considered her sister's words. "What am I going to do?" she asked them.

"Well, I certainly wouldn't put up with it, that's for sure," replied Medea indignantly. "I wouldn't let myself be ruled by an immortal monster and his beasts. I wouldn't let him gain my confidence so he could devour me at leisure."

"Please tell me what to do, sisters," begged Psyche.

"Kill him," replied Tanna. "You must kill him and regain your freedom. He has no right to interfere in your life in the name of love."

Although Psyche felt regret when she heard these words and knew their consequences, she was even more disgusted by the thought of being pawed by an invisible monster. "How do I kill him?" she asked.

Her sisters were quick to help. Medea was interested to know that his side of the bed bore no imprint in the morning. He must sleep elsewhere. "Oh yes," replied Psyche, describing the section of the palace that was reserved only for the staff. His sisters were jubilant to think that the monster might have a weakness.

"This is what you must do," said Medea. "You must prepare a lamp and a knife and keep them hidden before he makes his visit to you. Let him take his pleasure at your side and then feign sleep. Then, when he has left your bed to seek his own in the forbidden section, take the knife and the lamp and steal softly into his chamber. Kill him with the knife. See that you do it swiftly and silently, before he has a chance to wake and cry out. Then, you must flee the palace before his servants know of their master's death. That is the only way I can see that you can regain your freedom."

Each word Medea spoke was like that knife, gouging a wound in Psyche's own heart, but the words of warning from her sisters had displaced the memories of her joy in the Palace of Pleasure.

Chapter Seven

The Unmasking

When Boreas the North Wind carried Psyche to her parent's home, Eros had deep misgivings. Out of love for Psyche, he believed he had little choice but to let her go, and despaired of what might transpire in her absence. Once she was gone, the beasts came to him and asked, "What now, god of Love?"

He signed forlornly. "Was I wrong to let her go?" he asked. "Will she return to me of her own volition or will I have to call upon the North Wind to snatch her back again? Do I have the right at all to make her return to me?"

"We don't know, my lord," responded the Lioness. "We cannot fathom the human heart. It has too many complexities and contradictions."

"If I might be frank, my lord," responded the Crow, "the manner of her situation here, the wonders of this palace, and your very invisibility have added to her confusion and irresolution."

"I fear, my lord, that the words of her own kind will turn her head," added the Rabbit.

"Alas, I believe you are right!" said Eros. "But what are we to do? Shall we continue with our plans? Is there any of you who is tired of this? I release you from your contract, if it suits you."

"I'm willing to see it through to the end," answered the Crow. The other two nodded in agreement.

"I have to confess that I am weary," admitted Eros. "I have tried to play the roles of four actors in this masquerade. One player is my physical presence in bed at my mother's villa. The second is my spiritual presence as the Palace of Pleasure. The third role is as you see me now, spiritual essence assuming a human aspect. The fourth is that of the invisible lover, fated to enjoy only brief moments of love before having to rest from the stress of this melodrama."

At that moment, the walls of the palace shook, as if a thunderclap had sounded just above. "Then let me rewrite the script!" cried a queenly and indignant voice that Eros knew all too well. The façade that Eros had created crumbled to its foundation and disappeared, leaving a barren landscape. Then the palace reappeared only briefly before disappearing altogether. Eros found himself trembling before a power that was strong enough to blow his cover away

The ground where the palace had been was nothing but scorched earth on a bleak terrain devoid of life and color. Eros and the beasts stood transfixed, gape-mouthed and quivering before the startling presence of Aphrodite. She appeared over ten feet tall, and her sword and shield were strapped onto the short white tunic of the Amazon. Eros and the beasts dropped in obeisance to the goddess of Beauty. Eros in particular was humble in his demeanor. This was the mother he thought to deceive.

"I am disappointed in you, my son!" she thundered. "The roles of Gaia and her beasts in this deception are beyond my scope, but you have been disloyal as well as disobedient. And all for the love of this foolish, evil girl!"

At these words, the Palace of Pleasure reappeared and Aphrodite shrank to the size of a human woman clothed in the garment of a Grecian matron. As Eros stood abashed with his three conspirators, she paced back and forth, alternately wringing her hands and shaking her finger in her son's face. "At one time, not so long ago, we were fast friends, you and I. Not only mother and son, but friends! There was nothing that we didn't share. I thought you took a long time growing, but how silly my fears were, in retrospect. Now you are a youth, in love for the first time. And I am an enemy, the one who is keeping you from your love. Very well. You don't have to pretend anymore that you are ill. I'll let you continue to play house with that chit only if you continue your current relationship with her. If you reveal your identity to her, or if I catch the sun rising on you in her bed, I will end this charade and punish you both."

As she harangued Eros, he stood with his hands behind his back. Then she fell silent, staring at him with a gaze that demanded explanation. His cheeks were red with shame as he spoke. "Mother, I'm sorry I've hurt you. I know it was wrong of me to deceive you, but my only other choice was to defy you outright, for I am doomed to love Psyche. I couldn't bear to confront you and hurt you with open rebellion. Instead, I developed this elaborate plan, hoping to strike a balance between the two women I loved until I could think of a resolution. It hasn't been easy. Forgive me, Mother, please, and know that I have never stopped loving you."

She shrugged her shoulders in a gesture suggesting her displeasure and resignation. "Very well. I forgive you.

But my orders concerning your relationship with that girl stick until further notice. Is that understood?"

Eros nodded contritely, once more the youth under the scourge of his indignant parent.

"As for you beasts, you may continue your contract with my son, if that is what you choose to do. I bear no offense toward you nor toward your mistress who has long abetted my work with her husbandry." She turned once again to Eros. "Let me offer you these predictions, my son: I believe that you will have to snatch your mistress back from her worldly nest. I also believe that she will demonstrate to you beyond a doubt that she is just as contemptible and wicked as I have told you. We'll see what you have to say for yourself after she's let you down."

With that, Aphrodite's image became smoky and obscure, and then disappeared altogether. Eros and the animals exchanged glances and didn't speak at first, dismayed by Aphrodite's prophecy. Then Eros murmured over and over, "She's wrong. I know she's wrong." The animals looked at him in pity, seeing his suffering and uncertainty. They marveled that even the gods had the capacity for self-deception, for they feared the worst.

In the following days, the animals continued their domestic life in the Palace of Pleasure; Eros found that they enjoyed playing a human role. They had developed a strange friendship and treasured each other's company, knowing that time would pass and they would once again return to the forest. When that time came, they would resume the nature of their kind and be strangers once again.

Eros was happy to continue his manifestation of the Palace of Pleasure. Because of his mother's discovery, he no longer had to assume four roles. It was much easier to play three roles than four, so he had more time to assume his old activities. As he wandered through the countryside,

126

searching for opportunities to spread love, he realized how much he had changed. Each time he meddled in a love affair, he thought forlornly of his Psyche and the enterprise lost its zest. He spent too much time sitting on the window seat of his bedroom at his mother's villa, staring sadly at the hills and valleys below Mount Olympus, wondering how his Psyche felt and whether she would return to him willingly.

Days passed, and Psyche didn't return to the mountaintop. At the end of two weeks, Eros sadly called Boreas the North Wind to him. "Go," he said. "Go and bring my wife home."

Psyche had quickly re-acclimated herself to the ways of her village. Her parents and solicitous sisters made certain she was never alone, never without amusement or conversation. Her sisters continued to excite her fears and doubts about her married life, showering curses upon her monstrous and abusive husband and urging her to destroy him. Of course, she must not return to the mountain top, they said. Instead, she must defy him at every opportunity, making it as difficult as possible for him to use her.

So the last thing on Psyche's mind at the end of the allotted two-week vacation was the thought of returning to her supernatural husband. She wasn't thinking of him at all that night as she lay in her bed in her parents' home.

Gradually, however, she felt an icy chill. As she drew the covers closer around her, she remembered that her vacation was at an end, and that her husband expected her return. Deliberately, she clutched her pillow and tried to induce sleep and ignore the dropping temperatures. However, before long, she was shivering, and the insistent wind began to pull at the covers, whipping them away from her. Faster and faster the wind swirled around her, until it caught her up in a whirlwind and propelled her from the room. She was rushed by her amazed parents, who saw the door of their villa ripped open and Psyche blown out in a blizzard that carried her skyward. Higher and higher she climbed, unable to see through the blanket of snow that had enveloped her as closely as her soft bedcovers had just minutes before.

Suddenly, she careened earthward and landed in an icy snow bank outside the walls of the Palace of Pleasure. Wet and cold, her hair matted with frost, she limped to the door of the palace. As hateful as its sight was to her now, she was too miserable and uncomfortable to turn away. All she wanted was to find some relief from the winter blast that enveloped the grounds outside the palace. Reluctantly, she knocked at the door, almost hoping there would be no answer but fearing what would happen to her if there wasn't.

The door opened and all three wonderful beasts greeted her, their expressions a mixture of disappointment and pity. They shook their heads. Psyche's visit to her village had changed her heart, just as they had expected. They did not confront her, for they were beginning to understand human nature a little better now and knew that they would receive a suspicious, incriminating answer if they spoke with her. Instead, they directed their attention to her cold and wet state and offered her towels and a warm bath. They were not surprised when she waved them away. As she staggered away from them, they knew instinctively that she would have to be followed, that her unsettled state made her dangerous.

This requiring greater discretion, it was the Crow who followed, her broken wing nearly recovered, gliding gracefully and silently behind as Psyche turned away from the passages that led to her quarters and set off in the opposite direction. She had explored every corner of the palace but the southern wing. Although the beasts understood that the curious nature of humans might one day prompt Psyche to steal into the forbidden section of the palace, they had more to fear now, considering her state of mind.

Although she expected to be disgusted by what she might find in this section of the palace, Psyche was disappointed instead. The hallways were long and barren. Open doors revealed empty rooms with walls of stone. As ornate as the rest of the palace was, this part was harsh, ascetic, barren.

She was beginning to tire when she swung open a door and entered a room that contained nothing more than a window and a bed. It was so plain and primitive that delicate Psyche was once again reminded of the oracle's message and shivered in revulsion at being in the monster's lair.

She returned to her quarters, grimly satisfied. She didn't see the Crow at all, who was greatly disturbed and flew to report her discovery to the others. "The girl turned back after she found the Master's bedroom. She's up to mischief, for certain."

"Foolish girl," muttered the Rabbit, shaking her head.

Back in her chamber, Psyche set aside a long knife and an oil lamp. She hid these in the closet and hoped her captors couldn't read her thoughts.

He came at the usual hour, invisible but somehow bearing the fragrance of flowers. Before, this had been a pleasant odor, but tonight she reminded herself that the monster was deceitful as well as hideous and could feign those fragrances. He was kind and loving to her tonight, as he always was, but she cringed at his touch.

He threw himself from her with a sigh of consternation and sadness. "I knew that spending time with your sisters, in their homes, in the same old setting where they had spit their poison before, would bring evil," he said. "How true it is! I try to touch you and you back away from my touch, with less hesitation than you had when you first came to live with me in this Palace of Pleasure. Your sisters have driven you to believe as they believe and not what you yourself have heard and felt."

She could hear him moving about. Finally, he left the bed and she could hear the rustling as he dressed himself in invisible clothing. She said nothing, offered no words to stop him from leaving. She had the feeling he would have stayed had she asked him to. Even though he was invisible, his sorrow permeated the room. His voice came from the door, cold and distant. "I'll be back tomorrow." Then he left, closing the door.

If she had paused a minute to feel, she would have wept. But she had steeled herself for this moment for days. Even now, she calculated her next move. She dozed in her lonely bed for a few hours, waiting for the middle of night.

Finally, as the moon hit her face through the latticed window, she knew it was time to act. She rose, plucked up her robe from the chair and wrapped it around her. She slipped on shoes. She lit the lamp, took up the knife and left her bedchamber.

She walked through the darkness of her quarters and opened the door to the hallway leading from her wing to the other parts of the palace. All was shadow and silence; not the silence of innocence or peace, but the silence of stealth and duplicity. It was an inhuman silence. She was convinced that it came, not from her, but from the invisible evil within this palace. The gloom fell and settled on her. It swallowed her up as she moved from the main part of the palace, where the wonderful beasts could usually be seen by day, cleaning and cooking, to the forbidden and secret wing that was the lair of the monster who held her in captivity. Then a sudden cold crept in behind the gloom, bitter and biting into her fingers, which were clasped tightly around the lamp and knife. She thought that the cold came, not from her own thoughts of murder, but from the invisible evil all around her. She was afraid. She had to steel herself once again for the next few minutes, when she might finally look at the creature whom she had had in her bed.

She came to the door of the simple bedroom and gently pushed it open. Her heart was beating in hammer‑strokes as she raised her lamp over the bed, prepared to see a monster.

Instead, her revulsion turned to wonder, and her wonder to delight. There upon the bed slept a youth hardly more than a boy. His naked limbs were lithe and slender, and his hair fell in shining black ringlets. Two graceful white wings sprouted from his shoulders. His face was handsome, refined and elegant. In the harsh light of her lamp, he looked so vulnerable and young, yet strangely sensual and wise. He was the most beautiful being she had ever seen, and immediately she knew that this lovely youth must be the god Eros himself. With a sigh of wonder she drew nearer and leaned over to more closely view his face. But as she tipped the lamp in his direction, a drop of hot oil spilled from the lamp and splashed onto his shoulder.

He awakened with a start and blinked the sleep from his eyes. Gaining his wits, he was at first dismayed that she had disregarded his admonition to avoid this wing of the palace. But when he glanced upon the knife in her hand, he understood her intent and his dismay turned to hurt and anger. He rose from his bed, his eyes never leaving her face as he struggled with the pain of her betrayal. Without a word, he flew out the window and hovered at a distance, his eyes locked upon her face.

Psyche put down the lamp, dropped the knife, and ran to the window, reaching out for him as he backed away, a bright being against a dark and starless sky. She thought he wouldn't speak at all, but instead his voice rose scornfully across the void between them. "Foolish, treacherous Psyche, is this how you repay my love? For you, I've risked my mother's wrath. For you, I've built this dream-palace and enlisted those noble creatures to serve you. For you, I engaged in a confining, exhausting masquerade. All of this I did for love of you and, in return, you would kill me? Because you chose your sisters' words of hate over my words of love, I will leave you with them. Let your own cynicism be your punishment!" And away he flew, while she leaned out the window, beseeching him and calling after him until she tumbled out and landed unhurt on the grass.

When she stood up, she saw that the palace was gone. The carefully landscaped grounds and exotic flowers, even the snow and frost that she had encountered on her return, were gone, leaving a flat, burned-out spot of earth. The soft and delicate white nightrobe that had graced her body as daintily as a spider's web had been replaced by a coarse gray shift that irritated her skin.

Nearby, a rabbit, a crow and a timid lioness stared at her suspiciously. When she walked toward them, holding her arms out like a child seeking comfort, they fled from her as if she were a stranger. She was alone.

Sitting down in the footprint of the vanished Palace of Pleasure, Psyche wept aloud, conscious of a fancy that her contrite tears might bring back her angry lover. But no one came. Finally, she stood up and wiped her face, fortified by a new resolve. *He loved me once. He can love me again,* she thought. *I will search for him. Even if I have to scale Mount Olympus itself. I will throw myself down at his feet and beg forgiveness.*

But these were powerful words for a mere mortal woman who had no notion where to begin and even how to carry out her plan. She didn't even know where she was. For a day and a half, she wandered aimlessly down dusty country roads where there was not a farmhouse nor farmhand in sight to direct her, nor did she find a pool of water to slake her thirst or a berry or apple to satisfy her hunger. The glare of the sun burned her by day, and the chill of the air froze her by night, as she bedded down in the trenches at the side of the road, wrapping her arms around her and drawing her knees to her breast to reserve body heat, never really resting, never really at peace. She continued to cry in weak little sobs of self-pity, cursing herself for listening to her sisters and cursing them for hating her so much. And yet, even while directing her anger at them for their malice, she had to admit that her sin was deeper than theirs. Suppose that Eros had not really been Eros at all, but a horrible monster who just had the misfortune of loving her. She would have killed him and believed herself justified just because he was ugly. How was a creature like her fit to love, much less fit to love a god? Especially the god of Love? She had betrayed Love in more ways than one. She had shown herself unworthy of love, anyone's love. It was she who was the monster. It was she who deserved death.

In the middle of her self-chastisement, she was startled by the sight of a barn in the distance and a great expanse of fertile prairie. Her steps quickened as she forsook the barren roadway and stepped into the green harvested fields of the farmland, eager to meet the farmer who owned such lush land in the midst of a barren desert.

By the time Psyche got to the barn, she was exhausted. So far, she had met no one, nor did she hear the sound of animals or workers, and her puzzlement grew. Opening the great door of the barn, she saw sheaves of grain disordered and scattered over the floor.

Someone has come and disturbed the farmer's work, thought Psyche. *The farmer is most likely far away in a distance field. A malicious farmhand or an enemy has done this. Farmers work very hard and sacrifice much to provide nourishment for everyone. Who could repay the farmer with such an outrage? I have been so sinful that I wouldn't dare walk away from such sacrilege. Maybe the farmer will give me a meal when he returns, or will let me sleep in his safe, warm barn for the night. It's been so long since I've had a proper meal, or a proper night's sleep. And yet, even if he doesn't, perhaps I need to build up my account to the good. I've made too many enemies.*

So Psyche took up a rake and went to work. When she was done, she felt so tired that she lay down in the hay and fell asleep.

Suddenly, as in a dream, a tanned, stately and buxom woman stood over her, smiling benevolently. Her light brown hair was bound up and she had rolled up the long sleeves of her stone-washed cotton muslin gown to reveal strong and muscular arms accustomed to field work. In the apron around her hips, she bore ears of corn and sheaves of wheat. She spoke.

"My daughter, I thank you for your work here. These are my sheaves and this is my barn. By your labor, I know you are a pious child. But it isn't I, Demeter, the goddess of Agriculture, whom you have offended. Oh, no." She shook her head, her tender brown eyes showing compassion despite her words of reproach. "It is Aphrodite, the goddess of Beauty, who has a quarrel with you. Not only for the hurt which you have given her son, but for your own neglect. She expected you to be her grateful servant, having been blessed by her with a beauty that wins the praise of men and women. Instead, you took her gift for granted and substituted your prayers for indifference. Pride also caused you to sin. Your fortune is nothing unless you go to her and beg her forgiveness. Possibly by her good favor, you can win back the love of Love himself."

Trembling, Psyche prostrated herself before Demeter's feet. "Most gentle and kind goddess, I thank you for your counsel. But how am I to find the goddess Aphrodite? I am mortal and powerless. I have been wandering for a long time and I don't even know my way or where I am."

"Daughter, you must proceed to the east, to that very point of light which first bursts upon the horizon at the start of a new day. When you follow the light and find its glare almost too blinding to bear, hide your eyes and keep walking. The ground beneath your feet will give way. You will be taken up to Mount Olympus by the mists and set down within the villa of Aphrodite herself. Do not uncover your face while in flight, because the light will kill you with its brightness. Take your rest now and do not despair. Even the gods are not without pity for a sinner. You'll surely find help along the way."

"Thank you, thank you, worshipful and generous Demeter," replied Psyche, still prostrate, but now with a heart overflowing with hope and gratitude. When she lifted her face, the great and good Demeter had disappeared, leaving her alone once more. However, before her, spread out on a fine linen cloth, was a princely picnic, served up for her by Demeter herself. Long, twisted loaves of bread, fruit, nuts, cheeses and capon, fragrant wine and sweet cakes delighted her famished palate.

She was frightened, but at least now she knew she had a path to travel. It was much easier to know where to go than to wander in darkness. Psyche lay down in the hay for the most refreshing sleep she had had since losing her Eros. And yet, despite her momentary contentment, she dreaded meeting with Aphrodite. Not only was she guilty of neglecting the goddess during her brilliant days in the village, but she had hurt her son through her sin and doubt. She deserved, not forgiveness, but castigation and death. When Psyche thought of Eros, his beauty as he slept so innocently and sweetly, his gentle caresses and sweet love, she propped up her failing courage and knew she had no choice but to try to win him back. Otherwise, she would compound her wrongdoing with indifference and cowardice and miss out on her one chance for happiness and salvation.

She awakened before the sun touched the horizon. She could sleep no longer, for her dreams had been filled with the beauty of her lover who seemed to invade her subconscious mind as well as her conscious state. Even when she shut her eyes, he was before her, driving her on, giving her the courage to pursue her dream, giving her hope that she could complete her task and win him. Again.

In this spirit, she set forth, following the rim of golden light just breaking along the horizon. It looked so far away, giving her enough time to think about the task ahead of her. She was glad of the distance, for she feared having to approach the offended goddess, whose favor she would need to win her son's love again.

After a time, the sun came up big and bright. As she approached the edge of the horizon, it became larger and brighter until the glare was too hard to bear. She put her hands over her face, but that was not enough. She wrapped her arms around her head, but even that could not protect her from the light. She buried her eyes in the folds of her coarse and uncomfortable shift and crept forward. She was terrified, and if she hadn't been so set on pursuing this path, she would have turned back at once. She knew, however, that this was her only recourse. Her only path to salvation. Otherwise, she would be cursed, shunned by the gods forever.

All of a sudden, the ground gave way beneath her and she felt herself rise. This was how it had been on the mountaintop before her wedding night. This time, however, it wasn't as soft and dark as black velvet, but blindingly harsh and bright.

She was hurled onto soft grass, grateful for the feeling of solid ground beneath her. She dropped her hands from her eyes and lay there, dazzled. The world before her showed so many colors and shapes that they spun in and out of her vision. She thought she would be sick, she was so dizzy, muddled and blinded by her experience.

After a time, the world stopped swimming, and she gingerly sat up and looked around. She was in a garden where the sky was pure, ice-cold blue, and where clouds gathered below, eclipsing the earth. She knew by this that she must be on top of a mountain. And yet, what a mountain! The garden was paved with precious stones. A marble fountain poured forth liquid gold, and the flowers were as enduring as the immortals themselves, and just as alive and fragrant.

Just as she was regaining her balance and sight and taking in her new surroundings, a rich voice interrupted her reverie and shocked her back into full consciousness.

"Mortal, most ungrateful of all servants! Is this the posture you assume before your queen?"

Gripped by terror, Psyche looked up and beheld a tall and elegant woman with a flawless face and ebony hair that eclipsed the night with its brilliance. The folds of her gown, made of softer materials than a silkworm had ever spun, fell sensually along the curves of a supple and graceful body. This was indeed the haughty goddess of Beauty herself. Psyche staggered to her knees, shivering with fear.

"Why have you come here? Why have you sullied my property with your presence?"

"Most lovely of goddesses, forgive me," breathed Psyche, quivering.

"What! Speak up, muttering gutter wench. It is your queen who is addressing you!" snapped the angry goddess.

Psyche was so frightened that she could hardly talk at all, but she cried out in a timorous voice, "Forgive me, most lovely of goddesses!"

"Oh, so now it is forgiveness you are seeking? You think that pleading forgiveness now will make up for years of wallowing in sin? Do you think that asking forgiveness now will heal my son who is suffering from the wound inflicted by his treacherous lover? You false piece of mortal filth, you are very bold indeed to come here to ask forgiveness when a nobler creature would have fallen on her dagger for shame."

These words filled Psyche with even greater terror. Now she was sure she would not escape this interview with her life. And yet, the goddess, gazing into a crystal looking glass which she held away from Psyche, now seemed to abandon her fatal wrath.

"There is another way to escape punishment," Aphrodite offered, her features softening. "Repudiate your love for my son and I will return you unmolested to your village. Give up your presumptuous interest in him and leave him to me; I will nurse him back to health and he will forget about you, realizing that I was right all along.

"How easy it should be for you to abandon your interest in my son and escape my wrath! You can live the rest of your days in peace. They may be dull, and without my blessing, but at least you will be alive and unharmed by this unfortunate affair."

Shocked by Aphrodite's offer of clemency, Psyche was speechless, staring at the goddess' feet. Forsake her love? Return to a dull gray life in her village? She would be alive, but unblessed, bereft of love and its color and danger.

"Choose, mortal!" demanded Aphrodite. "Don't let me stand here all day waiting for you. What's it to be, life in your village or my punishment for your betrayal?"

Psyche remained speechless, trembling all over, frightened by her choice and knowing it would only anger the goddess more. Tears spilled from her eyes and gave Aphrodite her answer.

Aphrodite cursed her and stomped a foot petulantly. Then she said in a voice rich with disdain, "Very well, you worthless bag of refuse. You remain in my service, then, and I will use you and use you until I can find something of value in you that is worth saving.

"Since you are so unattractive, stupid and disagreeable that you can't be recommended for your beauty, intelligence or character, I must test your husbandry. I have a couple of small tasks for you. They shouldn't be much, even for a mortal like you. If you complete them with diligence to my satisfaction, I might consider softening future punishment."

Gratefully, Psyche once more prostrated herself at the goddess' feet. In her heart, however, she was less than comforted. To perform tasks for an angry and vengeful goddess would most likely require feats of Herculean magnitude. But, perceiving that she had no choice, she listened and prepared herself to do the task, no matter what the risk, even if it should cost her life. She knew that life would be worthless anyway without the favor of the gods and without the comfort of her lover.

However, Psyche couldn't see the looking glass that Aphrodite held in her hand. Had she been able to, she would have been consumed with love and shame. Mirrored in the glass was the image of the god of Love, Eros himself. He was prone in bed, propped up by pillows, weak and pale from his wound. The injury that he had taken on his first night in Psyche's bedroom at the travel lodge was purple and swollen.

During his courtship, the wound had begun to heal. Since that terrible night when Psyche had thought to take his life, an infection had set in. For the first time in his divine life, he knew pain and illness, which were unfamiliar to a god who is accustomed to always getting his own way and never sees the aftermath of his actions. Now he knew the suffering his arrows brought to a scorned lover. Neither his mother's ministrations nor his own tears could heal the festering wound. And yet, being a god, he couldn't die. When he saw Psyche in his mother's glass, he forgot his pain in his delight at seeing her again. He immediately wanted to embrace her from his sickbed, to offer her the forgiveness his mother was so reluctant to give. But this time, he remained the obedient son. This time, Mother was right. It would not do to take back the repentant Psyche untried. No rationalization for Psyche's actions would satisfy his mother's wrath and requite her wrongdoing. She had transgressed and must pay for her sin, just as he must pay for her evil and his own renegade love. He could, however, temper his mother's anger, and this is what he did now as she viewed his image in the looking glass, wordlessly beseeching her for Psyche's life. Aphrodite was in favor of a nasty punishment for the sinner, deciding that death was really too kind after all and wondering what horrible apparition would best suit Psyche. Rarely had any mortal survived such blasphemy and such insult.

Regardless of this, Aphrodite's love for her son was greater than her desire to punish the miscreant. She realized that her son might never be healed if she harmed Psyche. Yet, she wanted to try her to the utmost, to press home to her the price of her wickedness, to humble her with the tests she would give her. If she failed, or turned away in cowardice, she would prove herself to be a wretched creature whom even the god of Love couldn't save. This is what Aphrodite hoped for.

She pointed to a dark speck in a green misty valley down from Mount Olympus. "There sits my barn, heavy with the grain of wheat, oats and barley. I understand that you are quite efficient at farm work and have pleased my colleague Demeter with your industry. Therefore, you should find this assignment very simple to carry out. Hear me, wretch, because I am being quite kind to you, much kinder than you deserve. I want those grains separated and placed into piles by dawn. Get to it, for you have a full and busy night ahead of you!"

Heavy-hearted, Psyche felt herself plunging from Mount Olympus and through the green valley until she landed in a tumble in the green glow of lush farmland, scented with the fruits of the harvest, the property of the divine. The barn was about a hundred yards ahead. She was surprised that her fall had not brought her closer to her task, but gave small thought to it. Instead, she must walk to it. With every step, the lush farmland turned brown; the harvest of the lush summer had already been taken in. The landscape was preparing for winter. When she arrived at the barn, the sun was already heading west, casting shadows across the now-barren fields. The barn was quite larger than it had looked from Mount Olympus, and her heart sank even lower. The door towered over her, and it was shut tight. She grabbed the grimy rope attached to the latch and pulled. The door didn't budge. She tried again, and put her weight behind it. The door swung out as if moved by a more violent force and knocked her to the ground. Staggering to her feet, she saw that the door was now open wide and she had no problem stepping over the threshold to view the chaos within.

If the barn of Demeter had impressed her as untidy, this barn of Aphrodite seemed to be a sea of grain, scattered by a whirlwind. There was no beginning or end to the grain.

There were piles and piles of it, like endless waves in an amber ocean. She couldn't imagine where she was going to start or how she would separate the grain. In the barn of Demeter, she had access to tools to assist her in her task. Here, she had nothing. No fork, no broom, no shovel, no pail. The task was daunting, impossible.

Blinded by tears of dismay, Psyche wiped her eyes with her shift and fell to her knees, her hands sifting the grain purposelessly between her fingers, squinting in the dying light to try to identify one grain from another. She had made little progress when the light of day failed completely. Not even a lantern had been left for her. In the dim light of a quarter moon, she could hardly see at all, let alone see a tiny grain of wheat. She was defeated before she could even begin, and even her love for Eros could not help her. She wrapped her arms around her knees and wept for help and mercy. Her tears turned to prayers, as she hoped another divinity would take pity on her.

From the great heights of Mount Olympus, her truest and best friend watched with pitying eyes. Still burning with fever, Eros lay upon his silken bed and stared into the revealing glow of his mother's glass. He could sense the ardent spark of love within the maelstrom of emotions that passed through Psyche and felt his own pain soothed just a little. He sighed and lifted his hand.

To Psyche's amazement, tiny creatures began to mingle with the grain at her knees. It was so dark in the cavernous barn that she wondered whether it was her imagination. But, no, a few of the creatures crawled over her hands and she was able to see them better against her skin than when they were moving through the grain. Ants! At first, there were just a few. Then many, each bearing a grain. They seemed instinctively to know what was expected of them, so Psyche soon gave up any thought of helping them in their work. Instead she watched as tiny trails of gold, white and brown moved across the barn floor through the darkness, finally building great, gleaming piles of grain. She sat up all night with those busy little creatures. She could hardly see them, but she could hear them rustling as they attended to the chore. She wondered whether it was Demeter who once more was her benefactress, but she had the feeling that the goddess of Agriculture would not extend herself this far to champion her cause. It could not be Aphrodite, for it was she who set up the test. Could it be her love? No, she couldn't even give herself the luxury to believe that. Wisely, she didn't ignore prayers to the Ultimate Creator, nor to Zeus and to the rest of the pantheon; she couldn't afford to offend anyone.

By morning, the work was done and the ants were gone, leaving her alone and dozing on the barn floor, exhausted and relieved.

"Wake up, mortal!" The words startled Psyche awake, and she prostrated herself before the sandaled feet of the beautiful goddess. Aphrodite looked around her with a critical eye. She was dismayed and angry to see that the task had been successfully completed. "It is accomplished!" she exclaimed bitterly. She glared at Psyche, still outstretched on the floor. "This wasn't done by your hand, but by the hand of the unfortunate one whom you have enslaved with affection. Even now, he protects you. We'll see how long and how far he will go to protect you, however, when you fail him as you did before. You are not worthy of his love. You know deep in your heart that you're not. If you had any honor, any modesty, you would crawl back to your little hole and stop torturing him. You are not fit to have my son's love, and I will test you until I break you and make that clear to him."

She reached into the girdle at her waist, pulled out a piece of bread and threw it at Psyche. "There is your breakfast. You will need it for the next task. On your feet, mortal!"

Clutching the bread, Psyche rose up and followed the goddess outside. Aphrodite pointed in the far distance, where a grove of trees appeared. "Beyond those trees is a river. On the other side of the river, sheep with golden fleece are grazing shepherd-less. Your next task is to fetch me a sample of that fleece from the back of each sheep." She let a pair of shears and a large silk sack fall from her fingers and land at Psyche's feet. Offering no more instruction, Aphrodite vanished.

Once again, Psyche was alone and facing another superhuman task. It seemed as if the tests would never cease, that the rest of her life would be consumed on this black and murky path. Although she was heartened by Aphrodite's comments concerning her love's interference on her behalf, she wondered whether he was as weary as she by these endless obstructions and hurdles. She had heard stories before of Eros' capricious nature and wondered whether she would become just another hour's fascination, to be replaced by other interests when the burdens of this love became too tiresome to bear.

These thoughts almost defeated Psyche. When she viewed her prospects, however, she realized she had few choices, although her lover had many. She couldn't live having offended the gods. There was no other path for her but the one Aphrodite had placed before her.

So, foot-sore and condemned to this destiny, Psyche slipped the shears in the tunic of her shift, tied the silken sack to her belt, and began to walk toward the river. It was a long journey, but at least this time, the road lay through rich and flowering meadows and peaceful woodlands. Nonetheless, by the time evening fell, she hadn't eaten anything but the small piece of bread that Aphrodite had given her hours ago and she hadn't drunk anything along the way. Her mouth was dry, she was hungry, ill-rested and exhausted when she sat down in the shelter of a large tree. Her moment's rest at the side of the path turned into hours of restless sleep. The morning sun was already rising in the sky when she next opened her eyes. Her head was heavy and her mouth felt as if it were full of cotton.

As she struggled to her feet and sought to reorient herself to her surroundings, she wished she could quench her throat with just a splash of cool, fresh water. It was then that she saw that an unusually thick dew had occurred during the night. Drops of water sparkling in the sun fell from the leaves of the tree above her and gathered in the petals of the wildflowers that were around her on every side. She cupped her hands to gather the water from the trees, tipped the reservoir of water from the petals of each flower and slaked her thirst from the droplets nature's bounty had given her. They were enough to refresh her as she continued her journey to the river.

It was still morning when she reached its banks. Looking across its swiftly flowing water, she could see the sheep grazing on the other side. As Aphrodite had indicated, no shepherd was in sight, although Psyche suspected that the small thatched cottage sitting on a hill in the distance might be the home of the one who guarded the flock. First, though, she must cross the river. Although she could not judge the depth of the water, she could see in dismay that its speed and force would carry her away. Despairing, she heard hushed voices sweep over the water, inspired by the river god.

"Unfortunate," the voices murmured, "The action you contemplate is impossible. Even if you should cross the river, the fierce rams on the other side would tear you to pieces. Rather, wait until midday. The sheep will leave the hot sun to take shelter and sleep in the shade. When you cross at that time of day, the water will be still and the rams will be no more than dozing clumps of wool."

Gratified, Psyche uttered her thanks and sat down by the reeds along the river to wait. As midday approached, the waters gradually slowed until they became as placid as a pool. At that moment, Psyche stood up and walked toward the river. Saying a prayer to the river god, she made her way through the reeds and stepped into the marshy river bank. She could feel mud oozing around her sandals and between her toes. She had to struggle to break away from it. She much more preferred to stir up the silt from the bottom of the river as she made her way from the mud and into the shallow water. The further she went, the deeper it became. Before long, her shift was soaked. And then she was in water over her head.

Other than the impediment of her soaked shift, she had little trouble swimming to the other side of the river. The water was as calm as the river god had promised, and its coolness was refreshing and invigorating. When she reached the opposite bank, she took a moment to cup her hands and plunge them into the water for a last long cool drink before crawling through the marsh and reeds and up onto the shore.

Wringing the water out of the skirt of her shift, she looked up and around her to see the grassy hillside and the sheep huddled asleep in the shade. It was just as the river god had promised. She slipped the shears from her tunic and untied the silken sack from her belt. It was soaked from her swim in the river, so she wrung out the water and carefully aired it out so that she could more easily fill it with fleece. Then she folded it over her arm and approached the sheep with the shears in hand.

She walked as carefully and as silently as she could, not daring to startle or awaken the rams among the slumbering ewes. She couldn't help but admire these golden beasts, but there were so many of them, and each slept a foot away from the other. Standing yards away from the sleeping flock, she surveyed the scene before her with dismay. If she should brush against a sheep and disturb it, if she should lose her balance and trip attempting to step between each wooly body, might not the whole flock wake up and attack her? Even if she could clip fleece from the sheep, how could she know whether she had a sample from each one? The simplest omission might mean failure in the eyes of the capricious goddess. How could she possibly win? But, then again, how could she not try to perform this impossible task?

She stepped to the sheep closest to her, making certain that her escape path was clear if she should be attacked. Although the sack wasn't completely dry, she unfolded it and attached it to her belt, opening it enough to thrust her hand and a bundle of wool inside. Then she quietly knelt by the side of the first slumbering sheep and grasped a tuft of fleece in her left hand while she cut with the shears in her right.

The first sensation she had upon grasping the wool was its incredible softness. However, admiring its golden sheen, she was reminded of the pieces of gold thrown down by her father when paying for Tanna's expensive tastes. It seemed a shame to stuff this wonderful fleece so callously into a damp sack. Nonetheless, she had work to do and little time.

She put the bundle into the sack and gingerly stood up, meaning to turn from the first sheep and move to the second, but stopped to gaze in shock at the sheep she had just shorn. The spectacular golden color was slowly draining from its fleece. Before long, it looked like any other common sheep. By robbing the sheep of this bundle of wool, she had turned something that was wonderful and beautiful into that which was ordinary. What would the shepherd say if he found her here, shearing his sheep, devaluing them by her mortal touch? Would he be so forgiving to know that she was doing this task for her mistress Aphrodite? And would Aphrodite defend her or leave her to his wrath? And what of the flock? The first sheep continued to sleep, apparently ignorant of its loss. She worried whether the rams would be as restful when she came to shear them.

She stepped to the second sheep and repeated the process. Once again, even as she held a golden bundle of cut fleece in her hand, the slumbering sheep lost its color. She opened the sack to thrust in the second bundle, relieved to find that the first bundle had retained its golden glow, even as the sheep was drained of color. Growing more confident, she stepped among the sleeping sheep, shearing each one and watching the color drain from its body.

At first, Psyche had not been aware of the silence surrounding her, but as she made her way from sheep to sheep, she was impressed by the snipping sound of her shears. The sound seemed to grow louder with each sheep. Soon, it seemed as if each snip were as loud as a slamming door. She could see the eyelids of the sheep flutter, and one or two of the yet-unshorn rams stirred in their sleep. What if they should awaken before she completed her task? She had an impulse to turn around and abandon it before it was finished, making do with only half of what she had to gather, but she knew that incompleteness was failure. Once she had abandoned her task, she wasn't certain whether she would have the courage to re-enter that maze of wooly flesh. She had to complete the task now or she may never be able to do it again. She had no choice but to continue and hope that the rams would stay dormant until she had finished. The river god had not told her how long the sheep napped.

Soon, the noise from the shears was so loud that most of the sheep were disturbed by it. Some of them sighed in their sleep, others simply changed position, but, here and there, a closed eye opened, then closed again, as she held her breath and waited to be discovered.

Matters became worse when she heard an angry voice screaming in the distance. She looked up from her work to see a ragged shepherd ambling down the hill from the thatched cottage she had noticed earlier. She could tell by his gait that he was old and somewhat lame, but he was provoked to great rage, cursing her and waving his shepherd's hook over his head. Now she had even more reason to quake in fear as she tried to hurry with her task. She realized, however, that hurry leads to carelessness, and to the likelihood that she might lose her balance and fall among the sheep, jolting them into wakefulness. Who would be the first to confront her? What could she say to the angry shepherd, who had every right to know why his golden sheep were now shorn of their color?

Help me, she thought. *Somebody help me.*

The wind, which had been calm all this time, suddenly began to stir. At first, it was merely a pleasant breeze, but soon it was blowing through the trees and grass, masking the sound of her shears. Free from one care, she moved more quickly. Now she had come to the rams, and she feared these more than the ewes and lambs she had already shorn. However, when she plunged her hands into the soft back of the largest ram, he didn't move, and there was no sound from the shears when she cut his wool.

She was at the end of her task. Each sheep had been shorn, and each one had been drained of its color. She had not intended to degrade these lovely animals, and she felt ashamed of her actions. This angry shepherd was either the owner or caretaker, and she had wronged him by trespassing on his land and cutting and stealing his fleece.

Throwing the heavy sack of fleece over her shoulder, Psyche picked her way out of the flock. This brought her closer to the approaching shepherd, and she wondered whether she should flee him or talk with him. Her first impulse was to flee; he didn't look as if he were in the talking mood. He was shouting profanities and threatening to kill her, cursing her for despoiling his prizes. Her eyes were filled with tears as she turned toward him to speak to him; her only defense was the truth, and the truth was fantastic.

As she stood watching him approach her, the wind whipped around her skirt and tugged at the sack slung over her shoulder. With every step the shepherd took toward her, the wind rose in velocity until she had to hold the bag with both hands and with all her strength to keep it from blowing away. The shepherd continued to scream curses at her, seemingly unconscious of the change in the weather. The closer he came, the more frightful he appeared. He was a large man, despite his age and limp, with a clump of steel gray hair and a grizzled beard. His eyes glowed with passion and his face was twisted into a grimace that was terrible to see. Now he was close enough to hear distinctly above the wind.

"You tramp! You vandal! You thief! You worthless scum!" he screamed, shaking his shepherd's hook high over his head. She put out her hands in protest and surrender, but her motions of supplication didn't move him. He swung his hook through the air with all his might, renewing his attack when his blow made no contact. Then she felt pain as a blow caught her right hand and tore a gash across her palm.

Psyche had no time to examine her wound. The shepherd even now was pulling back for another swing. She tried to prepare herself to avoid the blow, but the wind, increasingly powerful, made her own movements futile. Instead, it lifted her off the ground and out of the range of the shepherd's wrath. He shook his fist at her as she watched him from afar, thankful to escape with her treasure and her life.

Once again, the wind had interceded on her behalf. It dropped her gently on a grassy hill some miles away from the golden sheep and near the road she needed to take on her return to Aphrodite. She was alone and safe again, with her treasure securely by her side. She was considering looking inside the sack to assure herself that the fleece was still there, but the blood flowing from her right hand stopped her and she dropped the sack to the grass. A long gash ran across the palm of her hand. She reflected that it was the same hand in which she had held that knife on her last fateful night in the Palace of Pleasure. The shame of this memory reminded her of the passion of her lover, the one for whom she had done this penance. Having come this far on his behalf, would he turn away from her at the end of her quest? At that bright, shining moment when she would see him again, would she find that his love was as cold as the pitiless blade of the knife she had held on that shameful night? Would he turn her aside, cast her away as a traitor to his love? Was it only a fond fantasy to imagine that it was he who had helped her complete the superhuman tasks she had been asked to perform?

What would she do if she were turned away? How empty and lost she would feel! She who had never before tasted love would be left with nothing but the ashes of burned-out passion. Now that the path to love was hard, not filled with the ease of the Palace of Pleasure, she found more love than she had felt wrapped in lace and solicitousness. Her feet ached from the blisters on her heels and toes. Her legs were cramped and sore. The sun had baked her once-flawless skin to a fiery red and every muscle was stiff with exhaustion. And yet, she was compelled to continue. It was something she had to do. She knew that she had little choice. She had seen the look in Aphrodite's eyes and knew she could not commit another betrayal and escape more severe punishment.

But that alone was little, she thought. She was really striving, not to escape punishment, but to atone, to show him some token of her love, even if he would turn away from her in the end. And if he found a truer, more lovely girl than she? She shook her head and prayed that it wouldn't be so, but if it were, she would not deepen her wrong with hate of her. Instead, she would weep and wish them well with a sincere heart; she was not really worthy of his love.

She thought of this as she watched the blood trickle down her fingers and onto the dust. She picked up the hem of her shift and cut and tore a strip away to use as a bandage. It was still damp from the river and dirty, but she tied it around her hand to stop the bleeding. She didn't want to stain the angry goddess' treasure with her blood.

Chapter Eight

Bound For Hades

Footsore, Psyche began her journey back to the barn where she had last seen the goddess. She had not been told where she should bring the fleece, so she could only assume that the place where she had left the goddess was the place she was supposed to go. As she walked, the weight of the fleece, dampened from the wet silken sack, bore her down. She stepped off the path to take a rest, finding shelter in a shady copse away from the dust and heat of the highway.

Beyond the copse, well-hidden from the road, was a sunny meadow flanked on all sides with trees. Here was the perfect place to dry out the fleece and wet sack. Tenderly, she removed the bundles from the sack and laid them in the warm grass to dry. The dampness of the fleece had muted its glorious color. Psyche worried that the brilliant gold that had made them unique wouldn't return.

She still feared the irate shepherd, but she heard no one on the road behind her. Even now, she struggled to hear a human noise that would warn her of the approach of strangers or enemies. There was nothing, however, but the chirping of birds and insects and the gentle wafting of the wind around the canopy of trees above her head. The fragrance of flowers and grasses filled her senses and put her to sleep.

It was a gentle sleep, rudely interrupted by a sharp poke in her ribs. She awoke with a sensation of panic and found herself looking at the shapely ankles of the goddess of Beauty who stood before her 25 feet high.

"Careless mortal, you dare close your eyes when you have my treasure?"

Psyche looked with dread toward the meadow where she had laid out the fleece bundles and let out a breath of relief to see that they were still there. She could tell that they had all dried because their color was no longer dull, but nearly blinding in the sunlight.

She got to her knees, trembling.

"What if a thief had come along and stolen them? How do you know even now whether someone hasn't crept up and taken one of them?" Aphrodite interrogated her. "How many bundles did you pluck?"

Psyche hung her head, struck mute. Struggling to regain her self-control, she stuttered, "I don't know, my lady," she replied. "I only plucked as many bundles as there were sheep. I took care not to miss any."

Aphrodite looked at her as if she were lying. "How could you know if you didn't take a reckoning of them?"

"As I sheared each sheep, Your Excellency, I saw it lose its color."

"What? What nonsense is this?"

"It's true, my lady. Each sheep became as ordinary sheep shortly after I sheared it."

"Impossible!" cried Aphrodite. "Go there in the meadow, girl, and fetch me my treasure. I'll see for myself whether you have carried out your task or whether you are lying to me."

Psyche crawled to her feet, walked to the meadow, and put each dried bundle into the silken sack. Meekly, she brought it back to Aphrodite and stood at her feet, offering it to her.

Aphrodite reached down and took the sack from her hands. From her great height, she could have crushed Psyche between her fingers. The frightened girl once again felt herself go dumb with awe. Once again, she wondered whether Aphrodite would kill her or torture her with an exquisite punishment.

Aphrodite took the bundles in her hand and examined them with satisfaction. Psyche could tell she was pleased by their beauty and texture. Nevertheless, her eyes were angry when she put the bundles back in the sack and turned to her. Psyche was surprised to see that she was angrier at her for fulfilling the task than she had been before when she questioned her about it.

"You couldn't have accomplished your task without a reckoning of each sheep, and even then, there would have been many chances for mishap. You didn't accomplish this on your own, mortal," she said.

Her tongue like clay, Psyche sputtered, "The river god advised me."

"How? What advice did he give you?" Aphrodite demanded.

"He told me to wait until midday, when the river would be calm and the sheep would be asleep."

"Is that all?" barked the goddess. "If you are lying to me..."

Psyche shook her head, although the rest of her was shaking just as hard. "No, Your Excellency. I swear!"

"I know that you did not accomplish your task on your own. What you tell me about the color fading on the sheep is impossible."

"No, not impossible, my lady," contradicted Psyche, bowing her head submissively. "The fading color told me which sheep was shorn and which wasn't."

"Ah!" Aphrodite understood. "You are fortunate in your friends, mortal. Let them do what they will. That doesn't convince me that you are a fit mate for my son. On the contrary, your actions have proven the opposite – that you are both evil-minded and ungrateful and that your very presence on Mount Olympus, let alone in the hall of Zeus himself, would degrade it. Do not think that your persistence in fulfilling my tasks has convinced me otherwise. It's worth a bit of discomfort when the price is a god's hand. If you really loved him, you would leave him, having already hurt him so much. Even now, you vain and useless girl, he is abed, recuperating from the wound his lover gave him. Perverse payment for kindness and love!

"I have been attending him myself and I know the sorrow he has endured. Day and night, I attended him while he called your name and wept bitterly. Even I, the goddess of Beauty, found it quite draining. I feel that some of my beauty has left me." She breathed a forlorn sigh, but then her mood changed as she found new inspiration in her words. "Aha, mortal!" she exclaimed. "I have another task for you. It is one which is easy enough for the wife of a god to perform. I have a storehouse of Beauty that I keep in the underworld. Go there and ask Persephone, the wife of Hades, god of the Dead, if she can give me a box of Beauty from the storehouse.

Tell her that I, your mistress, have lost some while nursing my ailing son. Go, mortal! Seek out the wife of Hades. But, before you go, here is food. The journey is long enough. You will need the nourishment."

With that, she tossed bread at Psyche's feet and left her kneeling in the dirt, feeling as if she would never rise again.

Tears moistened the dry bread as she ate it. All her efforts had served for nothing. The goddess was still angry. She still stood against Psyche and her love. Now this task was the worst she had been given, but she had received no sign that her efforts were serving to unite her with Eros. She didn't even know whether Aphrodite would stop giving her tasks that were more than a mortal could perform and were growing increasingly difficult.

What could she do? Resolved, she set out for a high bluff that overlooked the farmhouse. Standing at the edge and staring at the landscape below, she considered casting herself down. As she contemplated the earth below, a soft voice from nowhere chided her. "Rash Psyche, after having been helped thus far in your trials, would you now kill yourself in despair? What cowardice causes you to falter when friends have stood by you until now? Descend this hill and follow that road which lies beyond. When you see a large oak tree, surrounded by a broken wooden fence, take care to climb the fence and do not attempt to crawl under it. Then walk straight across the field to a stream. Follow that stream upward to the mouth of a cave. At that point, help will come from another source. Go now, and have faith!"

The voice faded into silence. Trembling all over but uplifted, Psyche began her journey.

There was nothing remarkable about her climb down the bluff and her dusty walk along the highway. As the voice had said, she came to a large oak tree and a fence. To her dismay, however, she saw no field, just a stretch of dark forest beyond. Nevertheless, she eyed the rundown wooden fence. It was as tall as she, and, under normal circumstances, she would not have attempted to climb over it. Because she was petite, it would have been an easy thing to crawl under it. She wondered peevishly what would happen if she tried, but, as she leaned over to gauge the clearance beneath the rails of the fence, she saw the ground gape to reveal a dark and bottomless pit.

The sight was so appalling that she almost lost the nerve to stand anywhere near the fence. However, when she stood up, backed away, and looked again at the grass below the fence, she thought she must have been mistaken. She tried once again to stoop below the lowest railing, but recoiled from a gaping maw in the earth. She stood up and took two steps away from the fence. She felt a sudden chill that belied the beauty of this summer day. Perhaps it would be quicker to go under the fence and fall within the pit, for it would most likely take her quite swiftly to Hades and his kingdom.

Plunging into the pit was too much to contemplate, so she determined that she must climb the fence as she had been instructed. She looked at it again. It didn't look like a supernatural fence, so she asked herself why she should fear it. Swallowing, she gathered her energy and threw herself at the fence, placing her weight on the fragile low rail to pull herself up. With a crack, the rail split and she fell in a tumble at the foot of the fence. Bruised, she got up and tried again, grabbing onto an upper rail and hoisting herself to the top of the fence.

It took her three tries before she was able to fling herself over the fence and onto the other side. The wind was briefly knocked out of her in her fall, but she staggered to her feet, squinting at the amazing expanse of grass and wildflowers before her. It was just as the voice had said.

The high growth of grass was so fragrant and the colors of the flowers so brilliant that Psyche was pleased to continue. They seemed to have a euphoric effect; she was suddenly taken by a strange sense of calm. The feeling increased as she parted the grass in front of her and walked straight into what appeared to be a rustic countryside. All around her was beauty. Forget-me-nots and daisies lay in a carpet on every side. Small animals did their natural tasks, as if they didn't know they lived on the edge of the world at all.

Finally, Psyche reached a brook, well shaded under the trees outlining the meadow. Fearing this supernatural world, Psyche caught her breath, thinking this stream might be like the river she had crossed to get the golden fleece. However, instead, it appeared that this was a shallow brook, knee-high at most, swift enough to fill the stillness with music of bell-like clarity. Inspired by the music, Psyche knelt in the grass to beseech the gods for success and thank them for her deliverance.

Thus refreshed, she removed her shoes. She wanted to wade through the sparkling water as she proceeded upstream. Sudden caution stopped her as she swung her feet over the bank of the brook. Reluctantly, she replaced her shoes and walked along the edge of the bank, stopping often to look for the cave. The dark shadows of trees and natural twists of the riverbed could hide the entrance. She might never find it.

Just as she allowed herself the slightest despair of ever finding the cave before dark, Psyche was frightened by the sudden sight of bats streaming underneath the shadows. They flew at her unafraid and circled her head, screaming in their high-pitched voices, trying to get her attention.

Psyche screamed and covered her head with the tunic of her shift, but the bats just flew closer, brushing her clothes and her arms with their wings. She was just about ready to raise her arms to beat them off when she recalled the words the voice had uttered. How dull she was! She had forgotten this was a supernatural world and that she had been told help would come from another source. The bats were not going to leave, so she must discover their intentions. She uncovered her head and stood straight. The bats moved away from her and hovered overhead. For a moment, she and the bats watched each other with growing trust. Finally, the bats gave a cry and began to circle the area. As their dance continued, they began to drift along the bank a distance from where Psyche stood. She followed them; that was obviously what they wanted.

They stopped at a place in the riverbank where deadfall and withered leaves made it difficult to walk. She had no desire to pick her way through the fallen limbs, debris, briars and tangled, withered vines which now barred her path, but the bats seemed to offer no other course. She lifted her shift to her knees and tied it up with her belt so that she could more easily slip between the branches, wooden stalks, twigs and tangles of the mire ahead of her. Covered in scratches and cuts as she struggled through the plant debris, she was suddenly heartened by the sight of a small, dark cave some feet away. No, she could not have found it without the help of the bats. As she crept over the weathered leaves and ducked under the stings of the nettle, she saw the maw of the cave open to receive her, to pull her into the darkness, the narrow, smothering darkness.

She had to stoop to avoid bumping her head on the low ceiling of the cave. Half-crouching, half-crawling, she felt her way through the blackness ahead of her, hardly conscious of the mud and slime oozing between her toes as the muck of decomposed plant debris gave way to dank and shallow water. All she could hear was the swish of water against her legs, and all she could sense was her groping hands reaching through the darkness and the cold water soaking her skirt.

She ached for the sound of another living thing to break a silence so terrible that she couldn't hear herself breathing and a loneliness so profound that she couldn't feel her heart beating, nor could she feel the sensation in her hands when she paused to press them together in front of her face. She was too afraid to cry out and attract danger to herself, but she wished she dared to cry out if only to hear something else besides the swish of the water as she slogged along, blind as a worm, now conscious of the smell of death and decay and the increasing confinement of the cave. She was dead; this was her coffin. Was she screaming? Did she hear herself scream?

For a moment, she wasn't sure. She was convinced she was dead. Suddenly, she was aware of a new sound, a brush of wings in flight, and she realized that the bats who had shown her the cave were still with her. It was a welcome sound. In the distance, she could see light, and as she pursued it, the water at her feet felt less like stagnant sewage and more like that of a refreshing mountain stream.

The light grew brighter, but as she approached, she could see that it gave way only to the piercing grayness of a dense fog. She supposed that even the dimmest light would have looked bright in the utter darkness of the cave. And yet, on second thought, she realized she hadn't left the cave at all. This was nothing less than a cavern, with walls so high the ceiling could not be seen through the impenetrable haze.

Psyche supposed this was her next destination, because her traveling companions flew away and she was alone again. She stood and looked around. There was nothing to see but the smoke of fog. All beyond was unknown and unseen. Abandoned in this atmosphere, Psyche began to be afraid, to give in to her fear as if to death itself.

By will alone, Psyche set off through the mist to the banks of a very wide, very still river. In the far distance, mountains appeared through the fog, still wrapped in shadows. Alongside her stood other beings, as smoky as the mist. They bore looks of detachment, anticipation, dread. These, she understood with a shock, were the recent dead, waiting for passage to the other side, and this wide water was the River Styx, the waterway that separated the living from the dead.

Within the silence came the gentle sound of dipping oars on quiet water. Charon, the ferryman of Hades, was approaching with his boat. Psyche could see the dreadful boatman, clothed in an immense black coat, hat clapped over a withered face mostly hidden in shadow, shoulders hunched over his oars. The journey of the ferry was long and slow, but some of the spirits pressed forward anxiously. Psyche watched them and wondered: Was death so preferable? Was the adventure before them so alluring that they appeared to be reaching for it? She was so single-minded that she hated anything that separated her from her love. Yet, she had learned that love made hard conditions bearable. However, if her love should no longer love her, then she, too, would want to turn longingly toward the river just like these recent dead.

When Charon reached the shore, he waved away the outstretched hands of the ghostly passengers who waited with her and beckoned to Psyche. As the ghosts fell back with drooping shoulders and disappointed looks, she felt pity for them, but turned her attention to the grim specter in front of her. "I have no coin to pay you," she softly objected, fearful that he would deny her passage.

The wide-brimmed hat of the ferryman remained lowered, but the shake of a lean finger indicated a large purse at his belt. He would say nothing more, but waved her forward with an impatient gesture. Because she was mortal, Psyche filled the boat to capacity and there was no more room for any other passenger. The spirits had to wait for the next ferry.

The ride across the River Styx was long and uneventful, filled with many moments of the slow lap, lap, lap of Charon's paddle in the water. She understood that someone else must have paid for her passage;, she wasn't certain who.

When they set down on the other side of the river, far away from the point where she had boarded, Psyche was amazed to be greeted by strolling minstrels and girls in flowing white dresses. Yes, the minstrels had a ghastly quality; they were lean and wraithlike, with empty eye sockets and bony, claw-like fingers dancing like the smoke of a dying fire over their instruments as they played a melancholy dirge clearly intended as a welcome to the earthly guest. The maidens were lovely, except for a deadly pallor. They curtseyed gracefully to her as if she were a great lady. They led her to a coach drawn by a team of six three-headed dogs. They whined affectionately when the girls approached and reached out to receive their caresses. The minstrels paused just long enough to assist her and the girls into the coach before they returned to their dirge on the bank of the River Styx. Drawn by coach in this dismal company, Psyche was escorted to a castle of shadow and smoke.

Wordlessly, the guards at the castle parted to let her and the ghostly maidens pass. They walked together through the dark palace, and, even in this world of death, the courtiers and ladies sitting and standing passed the time in conversation and in games. Psyche noticed that each figure was as thin as gauze, apparitions with no substance. And yet, beauty was still beauty. The clothing likewise was of extraordinary beauty, but faded to shades of gray. It was the exquisite finery of older times, full of age, but still bearing every bit of its elegance.

The courtiers and ladies who were standing paused and made way for her as she and her spectral escorts passed through the Great Hall to see the King and Queen of the Underworld. The object of every gaze, Psyche felt embarrassed and humbled by her shabby appearance. As she considered her muddy sandals, her dripping, soiled gray shift and limp, tangled, and dirty hair, she was suddenly shattered by a faint comment made by one of the ladies gossiping to the side. "There she is. She's the mortal who won the heart of the god of Love and then betrayed him. Look at her, punished for her sins! She's gone from being a great beauty to being as plain as a dish pan. How could such an ugly and raggedy girl like that win Eros' love?"

Accustomed to praise for her beauty, Psyche was startled by the words, but for the moment she pushed them aside in the single-mindedness of her quest. She could see the King and Queen, dressed in black, seated on thrones draped in black velvet. Hades, the kingly god of the Underworld, bore a scepter in the shape of a human skull. He was a horror to behold, with fiery red hair grown long and bushy over his shoulders, his thick brows nearly hiding sunken eyes that glittered like coals. Looking at him, she finally knew she was in the Kingdom of the Dead. Even the beauty of dead youth looked old and decayed in the shadow of Hades' presence.

The Queen of the Underworld, Persephone, glowed with a beauty made even more lovely by her husband's horrid appearance. She was unworldly pale, with hair as colorless as ash spilling over her shoulders down to the floor. And yet, her appearance was more ethereal than deadly.

Psyche fell to her face before the royal couple, trembling from the intensity of what she was seeing. Her tongue was heavy and she broke into a cold sweat. In this land of resignation, where the past is done and cannot be undone, Psyche's passions beat around the court like a trapped bird. She was reminded of her temporal condition, and of her state of imperfection.

"Rise up, much-tried mortal. We are in sympathy with your mission and fully prepared to honor the request of your mistress," said the Queen. She raised an arm toward one of the girls in Psyche's escort, who curtseyed and left the hall. She lifted her other arm in the direction of a heavy curtain of purple velvet. Elegantly, it fell aside to reveal a bath. "We are most honored to have the servant of the most beautiful goddess Aphrodite refresh herself from her journey."

"I am the lowest of Aphrodite' servants," replied Psyche. "And I am grateful for your kindness to me."

The Queen of the Underworld commanded her ladies to assist Psyche with her grooming. Behind the great purple curtain, they bathed her and combed her hair. Finally, they offered her a gown of fine blue silk.

Psyche was happy to see a color that wasn't tainted with corruption and decay, but she suddenly thought better about accepting such a gift and shook her head modestly. They then brought out a plain gray linen gown that she believed was more fitting. She was so grateful to replace her dirty old shift that she was glad to wear this gown and thank them for it. *Gray is a fitting color for me,* she thought. *It is a mixture of black and white, of contradictions, uncertainty and equivocation. This is my state and the state of every mortal, hanging always between life and death, between good and evil, between beauty and ugliness. I am no better than most of my kind. Trapped between heaven and hell and not fit for either.*

She looked in the mirrors provided by Persephone and saw that she was no longer the beauty who had been compared to the goddesses. She was common. As common as any mortal. The whispered comment returned to haunt her.

When she returned to the Great Hall after her bath and grooming, she found that the Beauty she had come to collect was waiting for her, shut up in a wooden box. Persephone nodded her approval of Psyche's change in appearance. "Mortal, I would not have you return to your mistress in the sorry state in which we found you. As her servant, we salute you and bid you well." She took the box and handed it to Psyche. "Here is Beauty enough to restore the loveliness of your mistress. Please give it to her with my compliments. Take heed. We immortals are aware of the vacillations of your kind and how easily you give into temptation. You must not open that box, but must give it directly to the goddess Aphrodite."

Psyche bowed before the dark couple. "I will. Thank you, Your Majesties," she said earnestly, and hugged the box to her for safekeeping. It was surprisingly light. Psyche wondered if Beauty could be so light. Nevertheless, these thoughts passed through her head only briefly. Now that her errand was done, the people of the Underworld seemed in a rush to usher her out and send her on her way.

"My servants will escort you back to the river," said Persephone. "Farewell, mortal!"

The girls in white escorted her to the coach and the coachman helped her in. They didn't speak to her or treat her as solicitously as they had when she arrived. She was out of place here; she was no longer welcome in the Underworld.

Clutching the box, she alighted from the coach on the shore of the River Styx and saw that the ghastly minstrels were still playing, although they had their backs turned to her. Cheron was already waiting for her, his ferryboat pulled up to the dock. From sunken eyes, he glared at her and motioned for her to hurry. He grunted at her when she stepped into his ferry, immediately turning his back to her and not bothering to ask for fare.

Her return trip was uneventful. Now that she had accomplished her mission, the inhabitants of the nether regions wanted nothing more to do with her. With all haste, they sought to return her to the outer world. She was reminded of her mortality as she watched Cheron's ferry slog through the water, heavy from her weight. She was earthly, not ethereal. It wasn't the world of Death that was corrupted; it was she. She lived, and had no part in the world of the Dead. She didn't belong there, and yet she didn't belong in her lover's world either. She belonged in the corrupted mortal world inhabited by her parents and sisters.

When she disembarked from the ferry, the first companions of her journey were there to meet her. Swarming around her head, the bats hurried her through the cave and back to the riverbank. Then, in a flurry, they were gone. She was alone now. It was late afternoon, and the grass and flowers that had given her such pleasure before were now muted in shadow.

Now, there was nothing left to do with this errand but to take the box of Beauty back to Aphrodite at the farmhouse where she had left her. In the shadows, gloom and silence, Psyche had more time to think. Her moments of self-congratulation were few. She remembered instead how she was helped every step of the way by the unmistakable hand that had always been her support. And by a host of others stronger and wiser than she, or more innocent and deserving of favor.

Had her love supported her through all of this? She fervently hoped so, but she didn't dare have faith that he could still care for her after what she had done. She felt certain that her benefactor could only support her through pity, not love.

How could he love her? She was not like him. She was tied to the corruption of earth, and her destiny was the Underworld from which she had just been ejected. Her corporeal self would rot and decay, and her spiritual self would one day stand on the shores of the River Styx, awaiting another ride from the ferryman.

Love is a thing that grows from beauty, not from philanthropy. After all, she was no longer beautiful. That was what the eerie gossips at the court of Death had murmured. When she had seen herself in Persephone's mirrors, she had realized that they were right. Her last vestiges of vanity slipped away. Once she, a mortal, had been hailed for possessing the beauty of a goddess. She had taken the praise for granted, never knowing how transient the nature of mortality was. Now it was all true: Hers was a common face, possessed by hundreds of young girls. She had lost her beauty in her efforts to win her love and now she was so plain that he probably wouldn't even look at her. What need had a god for the love of an ugly mortal?

Her tears began to flow, falling on the box she carried in her arms. She quickly tried to wipe off the wetness, but her tears flowed from her eyes so quickly that it was futile. Surrendering to her sorrow, she left the path and sat on the grass, the box beside her, and wept without a care. By the time she had no more tears to shed, she was exhausted. Using her fine new gray gown, now dirty with putrefaction, to wipe off the box, she asked herself just where her tears had gotten her. She was still miles from the farmhouse, she was tired to the bone, and these tears had done nothing for her but wear her out and remind her of her misery.

As she sat in the grass, blotting her tears with her gown, a new thought came to her. She had a box of Beauty at her fingertips. Maybe she could take a little Beauty from the box, and Aphrodite wouldn't miss it at all. Surely, Aphrodite, as lovely as she was, didn't need an entire box of Beauty to refresh her pale complexion. She, on the other hand, needed help desperately. If she should accomplish her tasks and then lose the prize in the accomplishing, what would be the use? She needed to remind her love what it was that had won his heart.

So thrilled was she with this idea that she didn't want to entertain the warning that Persephone had given her. Reluctantly, she remembered she was not supposed to open the box at all, but was to give it to Aphrodite straight away. Confronted with the possibilities of this new choice – the one in the box – Psyche turned to the box and picked it up. For the first time, she took a good look at it and wondered why she hadn't noticed it before.

What did she expect? Not this broken-down brown wooden box, scuffed, worn, splintered in places. Hardly the kind of container one would expect one goddess to give another. She examined it more closely, and saw that the latch was loose, and the clasp rusty. It certainly wasn't fastened securely. Why, she could have fallen and dropped the box! Perhaps it would have opened and let some of the Beauty spill out. Even though the box had been in her care, she could hardly be blamed if a mishap had caused her to drop the box. The goddess should have put the Beauty in a better container. She surely would have if the contents had been so rare and valuable that it required special handling. Perhaps this thing wasn't of great value at all, just another commodity that the goddesses traded, as when her mother asked a neighbor for an ingredient for a recipe that she was in the middle of making.

It wouldn't be a big thing, then, if she opened the box and took out some of the Beauty. If she took out just a little,

Aphrodite might not even notice. Excitedly, she took the box in her lap, lifted the latch, and opened the box just a crack, expecting that Beauty would flow out and restore the charms that had originally stirred her lover's passion.

Instead, a haze leaked from the box and swirled around her knees. As it swirled, it expanded to envelop her face, her head, and her body. She pushed the box from her lap and struggled to get to her feet, hoping to escape the smoky fumes that were filling her lungs and obscuring her vision. She coughed and gagged, vainly trying to beat off the engulfing gas with her flailing arms. The more she struggled to draw a fresh breath, the more the haze grew to overcome her. When it lifted, Psyche lay lifeless in the grass, the wooden box beside her, open and empty.

Far away on Mount Olympus, Aphrodite saw it all through her glass and crowed with delight, turning to her son who was convalescing on her daybed. "There you are! I told you this creature was unworthy, and this proves it. Even though she was warned by a goddess herself, she followed her own instincts and disobeyed her. What's more, she has stolen from me. She has taken some of the Beauty that was intended for me and has let the rest escape. She deserves the punishment that a mortal receives when she helps herself to the goods of the immortals. It is just that she should sleep the sleep of the Dead forever and never wait on the shores of the Styx for a trip to the Underworld. She is the author of her own punishment."

A stab of pain went through Eros' sorrowing heart as he thought about his mortal love and how pursuit of him had led her to this state. He had nearly been healed of his wound, and it seemed to him that his love's persistence played a large part in his recovery. Throughout her ordeal, he had helped when he could, but he couldn't save Psyche from her own rashness. Without a word of reply to his mother, he rose from the daybed, wrapped his belt upon his waist, took up his bow and quiver, and tried out his wings for the first time since Psyche's betrayal had sent him back to his sickbed.

He didn't have to worry that his illness had sapped his strength for flying; his despair had given him uncommon energy. He was airborne in seconds and swooped swiftly away from Mount Olympus, not even glimpsing his mother's amazed consternation.

When Eros landed at Psyche's side and knelt in the grass beside her, he sensed something more horrible than death, remembering his mother's fatal words. When he turned Psyche's face toward him and held her body in his arms, he knew it was true. Death was a temporary form of sleep, a door between worlds. The sleep of Psyche was the sleep of one caught between doors. She was dead, yet not in the state of mortal Death, where one door is closed and another opens, leading to the shores of the River Styx. Weeping, he laid her body aside and folded her arms over her heart. He stood up and looked for the remaining contents of the box, but there was nothing to be found. He picked up the box, closed and latched it, and set it aside as he knelt by her body. He removed the flask containing the sweet water of joy from his belt and splashed its contents upon her. He tried all his divine skills, but he was unable to bring her to life.

"You cannot wake her," said the voice of his mother. Eros looked up at Aphrodite, who had followed him from Mount Olympus. At this moment, she never looked more distant and divine in his eyes, nor he so vulnerable and human in hers. "She has placed herself even farther away than the Land of the Dead. She has placed herself in the Land of No Consciousness. She has placed herself in a place where nothing exists. Neither she nor you. And you cannot reach her. It was through her own foolishness that this has occurred."

Aphrodite waited, but Eros did not move. She saw him lean over Psyche's body, his face turned away from her, and she supposed that he might be crying. "Come now," she urged impatiently. "The mortal is lost to you now. Come away and leave her. There will be more girls tomorrow."

They were silent, immortal mother and son. Eros wiped away his tears and regained his customary spirit. "It is true, Mother," he admitted. "I cannot save Psyche from the Land of No Consciousness. But there is one who can. He is greater than you and I. I will take my petition to Zeus himself."

He impetuously turned to scoop Psyche in his arms and fly again, but his mother stopped him. "Son, take your rest first. You've just recently been ill. We will have the foolish creature carried to a place of safety out of consideration for the affection that she has inflicted upon you.

"Tomorrow, after you have rested, you can take your petition to Zeus and see where it gets you. You know how he feels about interfering in the mortal world. He makes an exception for an extraordinary mortal, but this one is nothing more than a pretty girl. I mean, she used to be pretty. So ordinary. So mortal. Do you think Zeus is going to grant a hero's boon to one as insignificant as she?"

Eros replied, "Zeus understands love. He is merciful to all lovers. So you always told me, Mother. Don't you remember? It is true that I have fallen into my own snare. Love for Psyche has tried me. I, an immortal god, have suffered immortal pain from her injury. Then, I knew the hopelessness of scorned love. I, who had before been author to many such relationships that led to tears. Yet, the weak, mortal woman holds me powerfully in her grasp by my own weapon. I must save her or retire to weep for a love lost while on the threshold of success. Poor Psyche! I must go, Mother. May Zeus grant me a blessing!" With that, he bore Psyche up and sprang skyward, flying from the grassy meadow so close to the mouth of Hades to the pinnacle of Mount Olympus, where Zeus overlooked the affairs of humankind.

Aphrodite's heart was softened by her son's ardent speech. She sighed in resignation and cast her own blessings after him as he flew away.

It was a small distance from Psyche's resting place to that of the king of the gods when one was immortal, but Eros could feel the fatigue, not being fully recovered. When he landed, gasping, on the steps of the palace, the servants of the great god fell at the feet of the god of Love. When Eros announced his intention to see Zeus, he was surprised to learn that an audience had already been arranged, and he was grateful and touched when the servants tenderly lifted Psyche from his arms. Together they walked down the corridor to the state room where Zeus would hold the interview.

Zeus welcomed the party as they entered, and Eros lifted the lifeless body of his mortal love from the arms of Zeus' servants.

"Come closer, grandson, and lay your precious burden at my feet," Zeus invited.

With humility, Eros approached the dais where his grandfather sat and gently laid Psyche before him. Then he knelt down beside her, ready to make his petition.

Before he could speak, Zeus broke the silence with a bluff and cheerful voice. "Grandson, I knew that you would eventually come to me to ask me to do what you shouldn't ask of me."

At these words, Eros worried that his petition would be refused. "Dear Grandfather, this is not a trifling thing I am asking. Surely you know about my love's great sorrow and distress, of how I lost my love at the moment of its blessed triumph."

"Of course I know," Zeus replied in a gruff voice. "I have followed it with mixed feelings. You know my thoughts about intermingling with mortals. Certainly, gods have mixed with mortals in the past, but most of them were remarkable for their piety, or their bravery, or their nobility. This girl has none of these."

At these words, Eros feared he must abandon hope. Zeus' brow was furrowed and his face bore a scowl of disapproval. But then, Zeus' voice regained its humor and lightness. "That is, until she began her trial. Strange creatures, mortals," he mused. "They are more pious in adversity than when enjoying all the world's blessings.

"Well then, shouldn't the gods employ their superior virtues toward the help and salvation of these mortals? Why not forgive Psyche and let her see the wisdom and mercy of the gods? But having her as your wife is quite different from rendering assistance and guidance. She is mortal and flawed. Nevertheless, you by your love (truly you are the god of Love) and she by her faith and courage (for these two are actually the same) have saved her from her folly and have elevated her. I would not be an obstacle to the fruit of love and faith. Go to your Psyche now as she lays at my feet. If you can revive her, I will bless your union and she will join the immortals as your wife."

Ardently, Eros kissed the royal hand of his grandfather and turned his attention to Psyche's lifeless body. She was as limp as a rag doll as he cradled her in his arms and spoke to her. "Foolish Psyche, once again, your own curiosity has been your undoing. Be thankful, my love, as I am. For the good god forgives us all."

His words brought the warmth back to her body. Slowly, her eyelids fluttered and opened. Her dull eyes focused on the sweetest face she had ever seen. She reached up wearily and touched his cheek. From above, Zeus smiled and extended his hand over the young couple, warming them and strengthening them as surely as the sun warms the earth.

With Zeus' approval, all burdens should have been lifted, but the fragrance of Aphrodite's presence reminded Eros that there was still discord in the family. He turned and saw his mother standing behind him. Her face bore no hint that she shared Zeus' approval.

"This is the first time you've defied me," said Aphrodite. "How does this happen to an obedient, loving son?"

Eros rose to his feet, ready to answer, but before he could say a word, she raised her hand for silence. "There is nothing to say about it. I know that you did this, not out of disrespect to me, but out of love for her. And she is a different person from the one I once asked you to punish. You have both been tested and you have both passed. By your love and faith, you have won your place in each other's arms. Zeus himself has blessed your union, and I cannot do otherwise."

Eros graciously bowed to his mother the goddess of Beauty and to his grandfather Zeus the greatest of the gods. Still lying at Zeus' feet, Psyche managed a smile; the words of Zeus and Aphrodite were potent medicine. Refreshed, she moved to her knees to prostrate herself before the gods.

"My daughter, save your strength," the goddess admonished. "I now know that you are my true handmaiden and have earned your place beside my son. Get off your knees and learn the dignity of a queen, the immortal consort of the god of Love."

With Eros bearing her weight, Psyche got to her feet. Gaining her balance, she bowed to Zeus and Aphrodite before Eros swept her away to his mother's villa to prepare her for a second nuptial celebration. This time, a wedding on Mount Olympus with the eyes of the world upon them.

Forgiven, redeemed, and revived, in the white light of the mountain, Psyche felt her fatigue, her human frailty, fall away, replaced by vitality and perfection. Even as she joined hands with Eros before the eyes of the immortals, she could feel his fortifying presence. His hand was comfort and strength. As she turned to view her well-wishers, she could see that all of the gods had come to the wedding, and were now rejoicing and praising Zeus' judgment. Aphrodite was there, no longer the steel-hearted mistress, but the mother of the groom. Joy made her beauty even more radiant.

The happiness at the summit of Mount Olympus lit up the sky. The credible old Pericles and his wife Leena fetched their two matronly daughters to travel to the oracle. Time had neither mellowed nor enriched Medea and Tanna; they often talked about Psyche, wondering why they never heard from her. "Surely Psyche must have carried out our suggestion. She always was a gullible girl. In that case, she is either dead, executed, or has fled. If she were still the mistress of such wonders, she would have returned if for no other reason but to gloat," they observed.

They remembered their last visit to the oracle and its predictions for Psyche. Had that not all come true? What message could the oracle have concerning the light in the sky?

When they entered the cavern to approach the oracle, they saw it bathed in a white glow that was a pale reflection of the light in the heavens.

Pericles stepped forward, and his heart was strangely peaceful. "Great oracle," he began, "we have seen a great light in the sky. We ask your indulgence to tell us what it might be."

With deliberation, the oracle responded. "On your last visit, you brought four women with you. Now you come with only three. Where is the young and lovely one for whom you requested answers?"

At those words, Leena, the placid wife, began to weep. The oracle seemed to take no notice of her tears, but instead waited for Pericles to speak. "Alas!" he said. "Do you not recall, great oracle, that you had predicted that Psyche would wed something inhuman? Indeed, she's gone from us, to be the bride of a hideous invisible monster who lives far away in a grand and marvelous palace. She has told her sisters everything. But that was long ago. Indeed, none of us has heard from her for so long that we are fearful about her."

Swiftly, the oracle replied, "Foolish man, you put your faith in me when the gods have already given you all the answers you need to know. The monster your Psyche wed was not her husband, but her own disbelief. You who will believe anyone who comes to you with magician's tricks will not believe the divine messages that are around you every day but do not come with applause or fanfare."

"Then what are we to know about Psyche?" asked Pericles.

"Know that she shared the failing of all your kind when she believed the wicked words of her sisters and thus nearly missed grace."

Medea and Tanna cringed.

"The fate of the long-tried Psyche is bound to the brilliant light in the sky," continued the oracle. "Come closer to me and see through me the splendid event that has lit the heavens." They drew closer and in the calm water of the pool saw a couple dressed and bathed in radiance, joined hand-in-hand. "There is your Psyche. This is truly her wedding day, and much more blessed than when you sent her up the mountain to an unknown future. Beside her stands her husband, the fairest of all gods. She is one with the immortals now. Didn't your simple villagers foresee that she was worthy of a god?"

Speechless, the group gazed upon the host of divine guests gathered around their daughter and sister and her beloved, scarcely understanding what they were seeing. There was nothing they could understand with their five senses. There was a point where their senses left and faith began. For some, wisdom comes at the cost of admitting ignorance and acknowledging that the facts are not available. Until they are, men and women must search for an answer, with their hearts and souls as well as with their minds.

Eros and Psyche turned from each other to gaze once more at the exulted crowd before them. Zeus and Hera, Ares and Demeter were there, as well as Athena, Hephaestus, and all the gods who had been spectators of the lovers' struggles. The river god was there, and Zephyr the South Wind and Boreas the North Wind, for once in the same place to acknowledge their part in the ordeal. A great gash in the mountaintop united the mountain-dwelling gods with the specters of the Underworld, and the bright eyes of Hades and Persephone blazed like coals from below the earth. From the center of the earth to the heavens above, Gaia's mighty shadow could be seen in attendance, and a humble rabbit, crow and lioness took their places as honored guests.

All attention was riveted on the newlywed couple, and all hands applauded when fingers, lips and bodies entwined, no longer separated by nature or necessity. When the wedding guests departed, Eros and Psyche came together again, lips meeting, hands caressing silken flesh. No more did Psyche have to rely upon imagination when she gazed into the brown velvet eyes of Eros, fringed by the longest lashes she had ever seen. Hardly daring to believe he was real and right in front of her, she cradled that lovely face in her hands and stroked cheeks that were soft with the down of first manhood. His hair was black silk between her fingers. Aching, burning, longing to consume and be consumed, she took him into her and gave herself to him. He responded by taking her into his arms and crushing her to him, and she felt the hardness of his body merge with the softness of her own. United in each other's arms, they were one mind, one soul, and one body, conquering and conquered, soaring triumphantly together to the summit of love's passion, each earning the right to possess the other.

Their trials were over. On the other side of eternity, they found their old cares had vanished, leaving a healing peace. All judgments and compensations had been made. In this perfect state, Psyche bore her beloved Eros a daughter.

They named her Pleasure.